NEIGHBOURS 2

Warm tropical nights, moonlight and strumming guitars. The Countess's eyes staring smoulderingly into his as he lit her cigarette, then, in a cloud of perfumed smoke, something wicked and French being whispered in his ear. Terraces and yachts, Wimbledon, Le Mans, the ski slopes of Switzerland . . . The life of an airline steward just had to be full of glamour and excitement. Paris, London, New York. Shane Ramsay thought it would be just the life for him.

NEIGHBOURS 2

Carl Ruhen

From an original concept by Reg Watson and based on the scripts of Coral Drouyn, Adrian van den Bok, Patricia Bernard, Sally Webb, Dennis Lloyd, Christine McCourt, Valda Marshall, Penny Fraser, Tim Page, Reg Watson, Christine Schofield, John Upton, Chris Milne, Wendy Jackson, Ginny Lowndes, Robert Guillemot, Rick Maier, Lyn Ogilvy, Hugh Stuckey, Peter Neil, Patrea Smallacombe, Kevin Radley, John Smythe, Jill James, Judy Nunn, Greg Millin, Bill Searle, Helen Townsend, Kaye Bendle, Roger Moulton, Bruce Hancock

A STAR BOOK
Published by
the Paperback Division of
W.H. Allen & Co Plc

A Star Book
Published in 1987
by the Paperback Division of
W.H. Allen & Co Plc
44 Hill Street
London W1X 8LB

Printed and bound in Great Britain by
Anchor Brendon Ltd, Tiptree, Essex

ISBN 0 352 32149 0

One

You wouldn't read about it. What had Maria gone and done? Turned up a *female* for him – that was what she had gone and done. A woman, a girl, who was expected to do a man's work, dig trenches, lay pipes, get her hands dirty . . . He shouldn't have left it to Maria. It had been one big mistake. But he had trusted her, respected her judgement, left it to her to find him a new assistant because he was too busy at the time to handle it himself. When she had said that she couldn't actually *hire* anyone sent out by the employment people, he had replied, why not? If that person could do the work, he had said, she should hire him on the spot, he wouldn't give her any argument. No problems, he had said. And that had been his big mistake, because problems was just what it turned out to be.

When she had called him and told him that the employment people had a qualified person on their books and were sending him out to the house for an interview, Max Ramsay had been blithely unsuspecting. Check him out, he had instructed her, and if he seems okay, put him on. Just don't let him get away; qualified people were hard to find. When she told him the applicant's name was Terry Inglis, he had still less reason to assume that anything could be wrong.

So, it was in a state of some excitement that he turned up at the house later that morning and asked Maria if the applicant had come up to scratch, if she had hired him, this Terry Inglis—and Maria had seemed to be quietly amused about something. She had to tell him

1

something, she had said, and Max's heart had sunk. 'He's not qualified,' he had groaned. 'I knew it.'

'I don't think you have to worry about qualifications,' Maria had assured him.

And then this strange girl had appeared from the bathroom, and Max was about to say something to the effect that he hadn't realised Maria had a visitor, when Maria had introduced this so-called visitor at whom he was now staring in growing dismay.

'Max, this is Terry Inglis.'

Sure, Terry Inglis—and it had taken a moment for the full significance of *that* to sink in. Terry Inglis— wasn't that the name of the bloke . . ?

'Hi,' said this Terry Inglis with a friendly smile.

He glared at Maria. What was she doing to him, for God's sake? 'She has the qualifications,' Maria told him equably. 'I was just following your instructions.'

Instructions, be damned. 'Him, *him*, I said.' He pointed to the girl who was supposed to have all these qualifications. 'He *can't* be a plumber. He's a woman.' Maria was still seeming to find it all very funny. Max wasn't finding it funny at all.

Then Terry Inglis was having *her* say. 'I've done three years at Technical College,' she told him. 'I've served my apprenticeship, and I have references if you'd like to see them.'

Maybe so, but this was something right out of Max's league. It was, let's face it, *unnatural* for a plumber of his standing and expertise to have a *woman* for an assistant. A girl like this with a wrench in her hand . . ? 'Look, it's nothing personal,' he said to her. 'No offence, I'm sure, but . . .' He moved across to his wife. It was just what he needed, something like this to happen at a time when he had so much work on hand, and he couldn't even drive because he was under suspension through just having done that after having a few more drinks than was permissible—and on top of that wasn't living at home after that blow-up he'd had with Maria who had just presented with that choice bit of information that Danny wasn't his own son, although he had been suspecting something of the sort for some time before then. And now a plumber's assistant who was a woman! Life was difficult enough as it was. 'It's your fault, Maria,' he bellowed. 'You hired her, so now you can fire her.'

Maria shook her head; she was standing her ground. 'You said you would trust my judgement,' she coolly reminded him. 'So, if you want to get rid of her, you'll have to do your own dirty work.'

Yeah . . . Max looked at her uncertainly, then at the girl who he just couldn't see in a pair of grimy overalls. 'Look . . . I'm sorry, but there's been . . . ah . . . some sort of . . . ah . . . mix-up. You see, I've already hired someone.' That should do it, he thought.

'You know that's not true,' Maria snapped.

Max glowered at her. She was being no help at all in this moment of crisis. 'What seems to be the problem, Mr Ramsay?' Terry Inglis asked him quietly.

Max was momentarily lost for words. Problem? She couldn't see there was a problem? 'Well . . . yeah . . . the problem is, you're a woman.' *That* was the problem, pure and simple.

'So are half the human race,' she coldly pointed out to him.

'Yeah, I know, but they're not plumbers,' Max retorted. 'You see, I take my work pretty seriously.'

Terry was staring evenly back at him. 'So do I.'

Max conceded that she probably did. 'But woman aren't designed for this sort of work.' He had the unnerving feeling that he was fast losing ground. 'I mean, they ought to be . . .' He gestured uncomfortably. Ought to be what? He wasn't quite sure; they were funny times; strange things were happening.

'Why don't you see if I can do the job?' Terry sug-

3

gested. 'You'll soon find out how good I am.'

Max was still struggling along. Both Maria and the girl were watching him with expressions of distaste. 'I'm sure you *are* good,' he said valiantly, 'but that's not the point. It's just that . . . ah . . . I don't want a woman as a plumber's mate.' He smiled wanly. 'I'm sorry.'

And that, he thought, should have been that, no come-back, his requirement simply stated, and fair enough. But oh no, she had to bring out the big guns while Maria stood by in rock-like solidarity. 'You'll be a lot sorrier if you have to fire me, Mister Ramsay,' Terry Inglis promised him, 'because then I will have no choice but to report you to the Anti-Discrimination Board.'

'And I'll be your witness,' Maria told her happily.

It wasn't happening. No, it couldn't be happening. But it *was* happening, and all Max could do was gape at them both. They had ganged up on him, these two, they had him cornered. Bloody marvellous. Bloody women.

It was still with this same feeling of entrapment that he reluctantly let Terry drive him to one job that afternoon. It wasn't a big job, and even if she could change a couple of washers without making too great a fuss about it, that still didn't prove anything. So he told Jim Robinson that evening as they were sitting in the kitchen, drinking coffee. Frustrated and angry, he had just been loading his problems off onto Jim who had listened to him sympathetically.

'Well, maybe it proves she will be all right at the job,' Jim observed.

Max was indignant. 'Whose side are you on?' he challenged.

'Women are doing all sorts of jobs these days,' Jim told him.

And making all sorts of trouble, Max thought sourly. *And* keeping him waiting. No sooner had Terry brought him back to the house than Maria decided she wanted to do some shopping, and now he had to wait until they came back with the van before Terry could drive him back to the bed-sitter he had rented since leaving the house. 'You think it's a good thing, do you?'

Jim sipped some more of his coffee. 'If it doesn't work out, you could give my mate, George Armstrong, a ring. If his son, Peter, works as hard as his old man, I don't think you could do any better.'

Max was interested; here was something positive at last. 'Finished his apprenticeship?'

'A couple of months ago, apparently.'

'Why didn't you tell me this yesterday?' Max asked reproachfully.

'Because I think you should give the girl a chance.'

A chance . . . Max grinned at him. 'Sure I'll give her a chance,' he chuckled. 'If she wants to do a man's work, then she can do it. Or try to. Oh yes, she'll get a chance all right.'

He was going to throw as much of the heavy work on her as he could, and there would be no excuses for her to get out of it. He would have her digging trenches and dragging pipes above the ceilings where there was scarcely any headway. She would unclog blocked sewers and dig out tree roots. Men's work—well, he would show her what that really involved. It wouldn't be long before she realised what a mistakes she had made and decided to call it quits.

But that was the trouble. She wasn't calling it quits. It was as if she had set herself a challenge and was determined to prove that she could handle everything Max decided to toss at her without complaint. she worked hard—he had to admit that. He listened intently for any sound of dissatisfaction.

'You're not complaining, are you?' he asked her late one night while they were working on some overhead pipes in a factory boiler-room, and she had just expressed the hope they might get the job finished that night.

'No. Just making pleasant conversation.'

This annoyed Max. He had been expecting her to complain about something at least over the past few days, and when she didn't he was finding himself becoming increasingly more disappointed. 'Never mind the conversation,' he said gruffly. 'I told you to put in all those thermostats and outlets.'

'I know. I've finished.'

Max looked at her suspiciously. He was tired, and he could see that she was also tired. She had just come back to where he was tightening the pipe joints with a spanner to stop the leaks and, putting down her bag and torch, had expressed the hope that they would get the job finished tonight—which, to Max, had sounded like a complaint.

'What? All of them?' He pointed the spanner at her. It had been a long day. 'Now, listen, I want the job done properly. It's worth a lot of money to me, and I don't want to be called back to fix something that should have been done right in the first place.'

She smiled up at him. 'I just watched what you did,' she said, 'and did the same with the others. I think they'll be all right. But perhaps you should check them just the same.'

Max felt gritty and sweaty. 'Well . . . at least you take the job seriously,' he admitted grudgingly.

'There's not much point in working with someone like you unless I'm prepared to learn—is there?' she said, and it wasn't only what she said but the way she said it that touched a responsive chord in Max. Yes, he actually felt flattered—and a little embarrassed a the same time.

It was almost midnight when Max decided it was time for a break. He stretched himself and wiped the sweat from his forehead. He was exhausted. 'Enough's enough,' he groaned, slumping to the floor where he sat with his back against the wall. 'Hell, we've been at it for ten hours, you know.' When Terry showed no sign of slackening, he snapped, 'All right, all right, you can stop trying to make a point.'

Terry put down her spanner. 'I'm sorry it's taken so long, Mr Ramsay, but I've just about had it.'

So she wasn't Superwoman after all, which was a relief. 'Well, let's take a break.' He patted the cement floor beside him. 'Come on, sit down.' Then, as she sat down next to him, he swore softly. 'I forgot to bring a Thermos. We could have had a cuppa.'

Terry reached for her bag. 'Coffee?' she said brightly as she pulled out a Thermos flask.

'Ah . . .' Max didn't like the way her foresight made him seem stupid.

'There's enough for two.' Terry was reaching into her bag again.

Max would have loved to have had a cup of hot coffee, but now his pride was getting the better of him. 'No, thanks,' he muttered. 'I'm not all that thirsty.' He hungrily eyed the sandwiches Terry was unwrapping. 'You sure came prepared, didn't you?'

'I didn't think a man like you would have the time,' Terry said humbly.

'Well, yes, I have been pretty flat out lately,' Max admitted, then as Terry held the sandwiches out to him took one after a brief hesitation. He bit into it. Roast beef, very tender, succulent. He hadn't realised quite how hungry he was. 'Make them yourself, did you?'

Terry poured him some coffee. 'I did spend some time in the kitchen, you know,' she said, and as he took the cup she was holding out to him, Max knew she was having a dig at him.

It was well past midnight before the job was finally completed to Max's satisfaction. 'Thank God for that,' Terry exclaimed in relief as, carrying all their equipment, they mae their way down the steps. 'I don't think I would have made it through another hour.'

A complaint? No. What did it matter, anyway? Max

7

didn't think he would have made it through another hour, either. It wasn't easy for him to admit it, but he did have a sneaking admiration for this girl in overalls who had worked so unstintingly beside him until the early hours of the morning. 'Yeah . . . well, you've got a right to be tired. I'll tell you something, though. You won't have to work much harder than that in your life again.' Suddenly, he thought of something. He stopped. 'Oh no.'

'What's wrong?'

'I meant to lag those pipes upstairs.'

'It's done,' Terry informed him. 'I mean, you were so busy with all the important things that I thought perhaps it would be all right if I went ahead and did them.'

Max regarded her uncertainly for a long moment. She was being full of surprises tonight. 'Yeah . . . thanks. It certainly makes a change to have someone who can think for themselves.' That was very true. Most of the others he'd had working for him had been absolutely hopeless. 'Oh, and don't worry about the overtime. I'll see you right there.'

'Whatever you think's fair, Mr Ramsay,' Terry said as they continued on down the steps. 'I trust your judgement, and besides, working with you has taught me an awful lot.'

And what uplifting words they were to hear, enough to give a man a new lease of life, a spring in the step despite his total exhaustion, a change of attitude. 'Yes, well, I know my job, and I take a great pride in it, and . . .' He broke off and looked at her with suspicion. 'You haven't been talking to the missis, have you?'

'Maria?' Innocence was written all over her. 'What about?'

Maybe she had, maybe she hadn't. But it wasn't beyond the bounds of possibility that Maria had taken it into her head to give the girl a few tips on how to handle Max, first and foremost of which would be to tell her that beneath that gruff exterior there really beat a heart of gold, that Max was Max, and that one of the most important things she needed to know about him was that he never liked to be told that he was wrong. But then, on the other hand, she hadn't been talking to Maria, and it was just her natural good sense that told her what was what.

'Never mind,' he said. 'Anyway, Miss Inglis . . .'

'Terry . . . please.'

'Yeah, well . . .'

This girl was making him feel uncomfortable again. 'Anyway, credit where credit's due. You did a mighty fine job tonight, I just wanted to let you know that. Not that I've changed my mind,' he went on quickly. 'I mean, plumbing's no job for a woman . . . so you've done really well, considering.'

'Thanks a lot, Mr Ramsay,' Terry said with a laugh. 'You're not so bad yourself . . . considering.'

Then Max was laughing with her. Not at all bad . . . considering.

Two

Warm tropical nights, moonlight and strumming guitars. The Countess's eyes staring smoulderingly into his as he lit her cigarette, then, in a cloud of perfumed smoke, something wicked and French being whispered in his ear. Terraces and yachts, Wimbledon, Le Mans, the ski slopes of Switzerland . . . The life of an airline steward just had to be full of glamour and excitement. Paris, London, New York. Shane Ramsay thought it would be just the life for him. He didn't think it would be any trouble for him to become an airline steward, like his mate, Paul Robinson, next door. It had been a piece of cake for Paul; Shane didn't think it could be any different for him. Manila, Tokyo, the Balearic Islands . . .

'Are you really serious about this?' Paul asked him.

'Do you think there's much chance?'

'Why not?'

No reason why not, Shane thought. Flying around the world, staying at the best hotels on their overnight stops, relaxing beside the swimming pool with a long, cool drink. 'Just imagine it,' he enthused. 'The two of us, in Paris, Rome, in London.'

'The three of us,' Paul said, turning over a page of the manual he had been studying when Shane had come bounding into the Robinson house with his bright idea.

'Three? Who's the other one?'

'Gloria.'

'Gloria who?'

'A girl I've been training with.'

11

'Oh yeah,' Shane said dubiously. 'And what does she think of you?'

'She finds me extremely attractive,' Paul said with a smile. 'Naturally. She's got excellent taste.'

'Oh, you're so humble,' Shane groaned. 'All right then, the three of us. That's if there's a job going.' He looked hopefully at Paul. 'Do you think you could find out?'

'Why not?' Paul closed the manual and stood up. 'I'll call the airline right now.'

For the first time since the accident, Shane was feeling confident again. He had just been given a tip-top medical clearance and was in great shape, fully recovered from the accident, even if it did mean his diving career was at an end before it had hardly begun, and that he was unable to do anything too strenuous. But a desk job was something he did not want; he wanted to do something that exciting, well paid and with a future—and as an airline steward he would have all this.

The interview Paul had lined up for him was a breeze. The personnel officer, a man called Finch, seemed to be quite satisfied. Shane's diving record showed that he was ambitious and hard-working, which was just what was needed. There would be another interview, he said, if this was warranted by the result of the first, and he was sure it would be, speaking for himself, but he was afraid it wasn't his decision alone—and, of course, there would be the medical examination.

'If it'll be any help,' Shane said, reaching into his jacket pocket, 'I've brought my medical report with me.' He passed the envelope across the desk.

'Oh, good.' Finch stood up. The interview was at an end. 'Then we'll be in touch as soon as we can.' He shook hands with Shane. 'And don't worry. I'm sure you'll be all right.'

But Shane wasn't all right. The news was telephoned through to him at the house later that afternoon. The interview had been fine, but he had been failed on the medical report. They were very sorry. They were really very nice about it. Shane was bitterly disappointed. He was also very angry. If it hadn't been for that stupid car accident and the back injury he had sustained . . . and now, because of it, bang had gone his dreams of the warm Mediterranean and bullfights in Spain. It was most unfair.

The fact remained that he still needed to find some sort of work; he just couldn't sit around all day, feeling sorry for himself. There had to be *something* he could do—but what? He studied the Positions Vacant columns in the morning newspapers with increasing despondency at the thought he was just wasting his time. Untrained and untrainable—that was him.

'You shouldn't be putting yourself down like that,' Terry Inglis reproached him. She had just come into the kitchen where Shane was morosely studying the newspaper that was spread out on the table in front of him.

'I'm not putting myself down,' Shane retorted. 'It's true.'

'Don't be silly.' Terry sat down opposite him. She had come to join him, she had said, because his parents were bickering about something in the other room, which was hardly anything new. Max and Maria were always bickering about something. 'There must be lots of interesting things you could do, if you put your mind to it.'

'Such as?'

Terry shrugged. 'Well, I don't know. You tell me. What sort of things do you like doing?'

Shane thought about that for a moment. There had never been time for anything else but his training. Max had had his heart set on his older son becoming an

Olympic diving champion. Now, of course, because of his back, that was impossible. 'I don't know,' he replied at last. 'I never really had any hobbies, or anything like that. Every spare minute I had went into my training.'

'You could see what courses are being offered at any of the technical colleges,' Terry suggested. 'Learn something new.'

'I don't know . . .'

'People are doing it all the time,' she said. 'Even in their sixties. Learning something new. I don't see why you can't.' He wasn't at all sure about that. What other people might be doing didn't necessarily apply to him. 'Besides,' Terry went on, 'all that diving and training must have taught you something else. Like discipline.'

Well, that was true enough. There had been enough discipline. He nodded slowly. 'I guess so . . .'

Terry spoke earnestly. 'That's something a lot of people don't have.' She gestured towards the room where Max and Maria were bickering. 'And you've got your folks. So whatever you decide to do, they'll back you up, regardless of how they feel towards one another.'

Listening to her, Shane had to concede that maybe there was some sense in what she was saying. He was beginning to feel better already, and when Max impatiently called to Terry that there was no time to be sitting around engaging in idle chatter while there was work to be done, he returned to the newspaper columns with an interest he had not felt since he had been so certain that he had within his grasp a career as an airline steward whose world would be his oyster.

While it might not have had quite the same exotic possibilities a job as a personal chauffeur was not without its interests. It was Paul who suggested that he might apply for the job which until that very day had been held by an acquaintance of his. Now, for some reason best known to himself, he was throwing it in, and Shane had nothing to lose by applying for it himself.

The name of the company, Paul told him, was Fielding Enterprises who apparently made just about everything. The job was well paid and not difficult. Shane was intrigued. It was definitely a thought. Paul gave him the company's telephone number and the name of the person to contact.

The vacancy hadn't been filled, he learned when he called the number Paul had given him, and yes, he could come for an interview. It sounded reasonably encouraging, but after his setback with the airline company, Shane wasn't building his hopes too high.

The following morning, he took great care over his appearance. He wore his best suit and carried the new briefcase his parents had given him for his birthday. In the briefcase was his medical report which, this time, he was determined not to produce until he was actually asked for it.

'How do I look, Mum?' He was very nervous.

Maria gave him a critical scrutiny. 'All right,' she said noncommittally.

'Oh, come on, Mum. I must look better than that.'

She smiled. 'Very smart. You look as if you should be having your own chauffeur.'

That was better; he needed all the encouragement he could get.

The interview was conducted in an office which had windows on three sides and abstract paintings on the remaining wall. Shane sat on the edge of the chair, his fists clenched, trying not to show his nervousness.

'Are you sure you wouldn't find this sort of work rather boring? I mean, there's not much fame or glory attached to it.'

The personnel officer's name was Thompson. His attitude was very warm and relaxed. 'I don't want fame or glory, Mister Thompson,' Shane replied. 'I just want a job.'

'But why *this* job?'

'I like driving. I like being out and about.'

'Fair enough.' Thompson nodded then stared thoughtfully at Shane for a long moment over the top of his spectacles. 'Well, there doesn't seem to be anything to prevent your working for us. Yes, all right. Are there any questions you would like to ask?'

'I don't know,' Shane said with a weak smile as he began to absorb the fact that he had actually been accepted. And with this realisation came a surging joy. 'Hours . . . pay . . . that sort of thing, I suppose.'

'Yes, of course. You'll be on call from eight o'clock in the morning until sometimes as late as ten or eleven at night. Long hours, I know,' he added apologetically, 'but the overtime should compensate for that.' Long hours indeed. Shane didn't like the sound of that. 'But then, of course, there are the times when Mrs Fielding is out of town and you get to have a paid holiday for a couple of days or so.' That sounded better to Shane. 'The salary is three hundred dollars a week, but it's usually more like four with overtime.'

Even better still. Shane grinned at him. 'Great.'

Thompson stood up. Shane stood up as well. 'So if you can start at nine tomorrow morning, the job's yours.' Coming around from behind his desk, he placed his arm around Shane's shoulders and led him to the door. 'By the way, a uniform goes with the job, so if you report to the supply department as soon as you get here, they'll fix you up with something. I'll let them know you're coming.' He took his hand from Shane's shoulders and opened the door. 'If you have any problems come and see me.'

'I'm sure I won't,' Shane told him enthusiastically.

'And don't be late,' Thompson said as they shook hands. 'Her ladyship has a thing about punctuality.'

His new employer turned out to be much younger than he expected. Somewhere in her mid-thirties, she was very attractive, very well-dressed, and very businesslike. Shane who, until she emerged from the house, and still feeling strange in his dark grey uniform and peaked cap, had been gently polishing the already sparkling limousine with a linen duster, watched her as she came down the front steps from the verandah of the house, carrying a leather overnight bag in one hand and an attaché case in the other. Like the house itself, set back from the quiet tree-lined street in this particularly exclusive suburb, she seemed to be the embodiment of wealth and style.

'Good morning, Mrs Fielding,' Shane greeted her with a smile and a rather self-conscious salute.

Ignoring his greeting, she glared at him. 'Where's Collins?'

'My name is Shane Ramsay, Mrs Fielding. I'm his replacement.'

'Then why wasn't I informed?' she returned coldly.

'I don't really know.' He opened the car door for her.

'I see.' She handed him the leather overnight bag. 'Very well then.' When she was comfortably settled, Shane placed the bag on the back seat beside her, then waited. She looked up at him. The attaché case was on her lap. 'You do drive, don't you?'

'Oh . . . yes.' Flustered, Shane closed the door then hurried around to the driver's side. Slipping in behind the wheel, he glanced up into the rear vision mirror. She had opened the attaché case and taken out some papers. 'Where are we going, Mrs Fielding?'

'We,' she said coolly and with precision, 'are going to Canberra.'

Canberra. Shane started the car. The engine purred gently as he eased the car back down the leafy driveway past the high hedge with the tennis courts beyond. Canberra. That was a long trip for his first day on the job, six hundred odd kilometres there and back, a fair drive.

'We're staying overnight,' she said. 'Surely they must have told you that.'

No one had told him anything. He turned the car into the street. Canberra. Overnight. 'No, they didn't.'

In the back seat, Mrs Fielding made a sound of annoyance. 'That means you'll have to go and get a few things, won't it?'

'Well . . .'

'They should have told you when they hired you,' she went on peevishly. 'They knew damned well I was going to Canberra and would be staying overnight. They knew all my appointments, so they must have realised I would need a driver. Any fool would have realised that. Unless they expected me to *jog* everywhere.'

'Maybe they forgot,' Shane murmured uncomfortably.

'All right then,' she said with a pained sight, 'we'd better stop off at your place on the way so you can pick up what you need. I do hope it's not too far out of the way.'

'No, it isn't.' She was riffling impatiently through the papers she had taken from her attaché case. Shane could smell her perfume. 'It won't take me more than a couple of minutes to throw a few things together.'

They drove the rest of the way to Ramsay Street in silence, with Mrs Fielding absorbed in her papers and Shane particularly anxious not to upset her further by careless driving.

'I won't be a moment,' he said when he pulled up outside his house a little less than half an hour later.

'Fine.'

Leaving her there with her papers, Shane hurried into the house. His father was home. 'Well, well, well,' he said, coming out of the kitchen as Shane headed towards his bedroom. 'What have we here? The grey ghost?'

'No jokes, Dad. I'm in a hurry.'

'All right, all right, keep your hair on.' Max disappeared back into the kitchen.

Shane was just about to enter his room when there was a knock at the front door. He doubled back to open it. Mrs Fielding was standing there. 'I need to use your telephone.'

'Sure, go ahead.' He pointed to the telephone in the hall. 'I'll only be a minute.'

As he gathered a few things together and shoved them into a bag, he could hear her in the hall complaining to someone at the other end of the line about her car telephone which still hadn't been fixed, and there would be hell to pay about *that*, when she got back, she promised. But in the meantime, she wanted to know if the hotel reservations in Canberra had been made. 'For two. For one night. Yes, that's right . . . two . . . and the name is Ramsay. Shane Ramsay.'

Max must have heard it as well, because the next thing Shane heard was his father's voice out in the hall, demanding what the hell was going *on* here. Oh no, Shane groaned in dismay, and rushed back out into the hall where Mrs Fielding, one hand covering the mouthpiece of the receiver was looking at Max with the curiosity one might expect from a scientist studying a rare and not particularly attractive form of insect life. For his part, Max was just looking belligerent.

'Dad, she's my boss.'

'Yeah?' Max growled, looking from one of them to the other. 'You don't go to hotels with your boss.'

'It's a business trip, Dad.' It was just what he needed, on his very first day, something like this to happen. His job at an end before it had even properly begun. He turned to the woman standing rather imperiously beside the telephone table. 'Mrs Fielding, this is my Dad.' He turned to his father. 'Dad, this is Mrs Fielding . . . my new boss.' he gave it special emphasis. He had already been embarrassed quite enough by his father's charging in like a bull in a china shop.

'Yeah . . .' Shane could tell that his father was still suspicious.

'If it's all right with you, Mister Ramsay,' Mrs Fielding said coolly, 'I would like to finish my telephone call.

'I suppose so,' Max said, still doubtfully.

'Thank you.' Mrs Fielding pointedly turned her back on him and resumed her telephone conversation.

Max was glaring at Shane. 'I want a word with you,' he said in a tone that bode well for no one, least of all Shane.

'Not here.' Shane cast a quick glance at Mrs Fielding, then led the way into the kitchen. 'Jeez, Dad, what the hell do you think you're doing?' he demanded angrily. 'Trying to make me lose my job?'

'If that's what you have to keep a job,' Max said in disgust, 'then it's not worth having, son.'

Honestly, there was no getting through to him. Shane was becoming totally exasperated. 'Look, will you cut it out, and listen.' It was only with difficulty that he managed to keep his voice down. 'I'm Mrs Fielding's *chauffeur*—don't you understand? I'm taking her to Canberra. She has business down there, and we're staying overnight—hence the hotel reservations. That's all it is, Dad, so cool it, will you?'

He could tell he was getting through to him because now Max was looking somewhat abashed. 'Ah . . . I suppose that's all right.'

All right? Of course it was all right. 'Good.' Shane turned away. They had wasted enough time. 'Now I've got to finish my packing.' Mrs Fielding was still on the telephone, crisply giving orders as he passed her in the hall on the way to his bedroom.

She had finished her telephone conversation by the

time he emerged again from his room. Now she was looking bored as Max regaled her in the living room with no doubt glowing reports of his son, the former Olympic hopeful turned uniformed chauffeur—and that was just as embarrassing. 'I was telling Mrs Fielding what a great diver you were.'

'We're late, Dad,' Shane said brusquely. 'I'll see you.'

'Well . . . have a good time.'

'Goodbye, Dad.'

'Is your father always like that?' Mrs Fielding asked suddenly after they had been driving for about twenty minutes.

Startled by the abruptness of the question, Shane glanced up at the rear-view mirror. She had all her papers out again; she would probably be fully occupied with them all the way to Canberra. 'Like what?'

'Jumping to outrageous conclusions.'

'Mostly.' Shane smiled. 'But he doesn't mean anything. His bark is far worse than his bite.' Yes, that summed him up quite nicely.

'There are a lot of people like that,' Mrs Fielding observed, and Shane wondered just how poisonous her own bite could be.

There was another silence, another riffle of papers. Suburban bungalows slid silently away on either side. Soon they would be on the freeway. It would take them about three hours to reach Canberra.

'He was saying you could have been an Olympic diving champion,' she remarked, and Shane could feel the sudden warmth in his cheeks. That bloody father of his . . . He'd had such high hopes.

'He was exaggerating. I won a few trophies, that was all.' He could see the freeway sign in the distance.

'How many is a few?'

'Well . . . I *was* training for the Olympics,' he said self-consciously. 'But there was no guarantee that I was going to make it.'

'But you must have shown some promise.'

'I suppose . . .' Two more kilometres to the freeway. Shane was beginning to feel more relaxed with this woman who, it seemed, was not quite so distant and unfriendly as he had at first thought. 'Well, some . . . yes.'

'Then why did you give it up?'

'I had no choice, really. An accident. I injured my back. It's okay now, but I can't do any more diving.'

'That's a shame,' she said sympathetically from the back seat. 'What happened?'

'A car accident. It wasn't my fault. This guy ran into me and my brother. We were lucky we weren't both killed.'

'All right, that's enough,' Mrs Fielding said sharply.

Taken aback by the abrupt change of tone, Shane cast another quick glance at her in the rear-view mirror. She was studying her papers again. 'I thought you were interested.'

'Not in your life story,' she snapped without looking up from her papers—and it was as if an invisible wall had suddenly been thrown up between them. Shane was bewildered. What had he said to make her suddenly close herself off like that? One more kilometre to the freeway. It was going to be a long silent drive to Canberra.

As it turned out, it was not only a long silent drive to Canberra, but a long silent drive back again. She spoke only to give him orders. She was very distant—and Shane wondered over and over again what it was, if anything, he had said to upset her.

One morning, about a week later, he was waiting with the car outside her house when he found himself in conversation with the gardener who asked him how he liked working for Mrs Fielding. 'Don't ask,' he replied. 'I was two minutes late for work last night. She nearly bit my head off.' It wasn't the first time she had hauled

22

him over the coals for being late. She had a very sharp tongue.

'Oh yes,' the gardener said with a laugh. 'That temper of hers . . .'

'What about her husband?' It was something Shane had been wondering about for some days now. There was one somewhere, he knew, but no one seemed to know anything about him—or was willing to talk about him. 'Is he the same?'

The gardener was leaning on his rake. He was a man somewhere in his sixties with a prickly grey stubble on his jaw. 'I wouldn't know. I haven't met him. I've only been here a couple of months.' He looked at Shane shrewdly for a moment. 'Mind you, I've heard the odd rumour or two,' he said confidentially. 'Mightn't be anything to them, of course.'

'But then again?' Shane was curious.

'Then again.' The gardener moved closer to him, and nodded towards the house. 'Apparently she was his private secretary. She's much younger than he is, but she always had an eye open for the big chance—that's what I heard, anyway. She spotted all that money, and bingo, up to the altar they went, thanks very much.'

Shane laughed. 'I can think of harder ways to come into a few million.'

'Yes.' The gardener nodded slowly, conspiratorially. 'The thing is, though, she just didn't get her hooks into the money. She got her hooks into the company as well. As far as I can see, she's the only one running the business now.'

'And what about him?'

'Who knows?' The gardener laughed again. 'Maybe she shot him.'

Maybe she did. There was nothing about that woman that would have surprised Shane. 'I wouldn't put it past her,' he remarked drily.

Then, alerted by a soft, discreet cough from the

gardener, he turned to see Mrs Fielding coming down the steps from the house as the gardener went back to raking up leaves on the lawn. The smile faded from Shane's face; he was suddenly businesslike and alert again. He saluted and opened the car door for her. 'Good morning, Mrs Fielding. To the office?'

'No,' she said as she stepped into the car. 'To the Norwood Private Hospital.'

He gently closed the door after her and moved around to the driver's side. The Norwood Private Hospital? Why there, for Heaven's sake? This was becoming stranger all the time.

The Norwood Private Hospital was surrounded by trees and extensive lawns trimmed and dotted with flowerbeds that displayed a riot of colour. The place looked very exclusive—and expensive. 'You can take the afternoon off,' Mrs Fielding said as she stepped out of the car and looked up at the porticoed entrance to the building with an air of steeling herself for an ordeal to come. 'Come and pick me up at six-thirty.'

Shane closed the car door. 'Whereabouts in the hospital will I find you?'

She turned to face him. 'I want you to wait out here.' Her blue eyes regarded him coldly. 'In fact,' she went on, 'if you so much as set one foot inside that hospital, you can consider yourself fired.' She had said it quite matter-of-factly, but there had been no mistaking the steely edge to her tone. Very curious indeed, Shane thought as he watched her move up the front steps to the hospital entrance.

That evening, he was back at the hospital with plenty of time to spare. He settled to down to wait. After about five minutes, the car telephone rang. He picked up the receiver.

'Peterson here,' a male voice informed brusquely. 'I want to speak to Mrs Fielding.'

Shane glanced up at the windows of the hospital

which were reflecting the light from the lowering sun. 'Mrs Fielding is not available at the moment. Can I take a message?'

'It's urgent.' Peterson was one of the company's top executives. 'Do you know where you can find her?'

'Yes, but she left strict instructions not to be disturbed.'

'You don't understand,' the man growled at the other end of the line. 'This is very important.'

Shane felt suddenly cornered. If this guy Peterson was going to make an issue of it . . . Shane glanced at his watch. 'She won't be more than twenty minutes.' A stickler for punctuality, it would be twenty minutes on the dot. 'Can I get her to call you back?'

'No, you can't,' Peterson snapped. 'You find her right now and get her to call me. Have you got that?'

'Yes,' Shane said unhappily, and replaced the receiver.

With a sigh he looked up again at the windows that were reflecting the sunlight. She had meant what she said about him not setting a foot inside the hospital. He didn't doubt that it would cost him his job if he did, as he didn't doubt it would cost him his job if he didn't, if the matter was as important as Peterson had made out. He opened the car door and stepped out onto the pink gravel driveway. There was nothing else for it . . . Full of trepidation, he climbed the steps to the entrance of the hospital which Mrs Fielding, blast her, had forbidden him to enter under pain of losing the job which, all things considered, and despite Mrs Fielding herself, was suiting him rather well.

Inside the hospital, with its dark rich panelling and the smell of furniture polish, he was directed to a room on the first floor. The door of the room was partly open. Shane was about to knock on the door when he heard voices coming from inside the room. He hesitated. He heard Mrs Fielding's voice, softer and more concerned than he was accustomed to hearing it.

25

'Now, really, Dan, you've got to stop worrying about the business,' she was saying. 'That's what put you in here in the first place. Everything's fine—the new accounts, everything.'

The man's voice was barely audible. He sounded very weary. 'Yes, darling. Yes . . . I knew I could count on you. But . . . I'm sorry, Linda . . . the way things have turned out. You being tied to a useless old man like me. Such a waste . . .'

'Don't be silly, Dan. You mustn't talk like that.'

In the corridor, Shane stood beside the partly open door, listening to the voices that were coming from inside the room. Apart from her voice, which was unmistakably hers, it could have been another woman altogether.

'I'm a lucky man, Linda,' the man's cracked tired voice went on. 'It if hadn't been for you, I . . . I would never have pulled through all those operations.'

'Of course you would,' Mrs Fielding assured him. 'Bu the way, did Doctor Williams tell you the good news?'

'That I could go home soon?'

'Yes.'

'Perhaps,' the man said doubtfully. 'But I think he was only trying to bolster my spirits.'

'That's not true. You'll be out of here in a couple of weeks. The beach house is ready. I've been bullying the tradesmen for months now so they would have it finished in time. All it needs now is us to be living in it.'

Feeling that he had overheard too much already, that he was an intruder who had no right to be there, Shane tapped softly on the door and pushed it further open. 'I'm sorry to trouble you, Mrs Fielding . . .'

She was sitting on a chair beside the bed. In the bed, sitting up, with pillows propped behind him, was an old man with wispy white hair and a drawn, very pale face. Seeing Shane, Mrs Fielding's own face immediately hardened. She sprang to her feet. 'What are you doing here?' she demanded angrily. 'I told you to wait for me outside.' She turned to the old man in the bed. 'I'm sorry, Dan. I'll be back in a moment.' She followed Shane out in the corridor, closing the door behind her. 'What the hell do you think you're doing?' she hissed, and Shane thought miserably that this was more like the woman he knew, the unrelenting boss who he had thought would be too busy making money to waste time sitting beside the hospital bed of a sick old man with wispy white hair and telling him that the beach house was ready for them both to occupy. 'I thought I made it perfectly clear that you were to wait for me in the car.' She was obviously very angry. Her eyes bore into his like gimlets.

'I know . . . but Mister Peterson rang . . . he insisted . . .'

'And who gives you your instructions? Mister Peterson, or me.'

'You do.'

She glanced at the closed door of the room they had just left. 'My husband has been very ill,' she told Shane. 'When I come to visit him, *nothing* gets in the way of our spending a few precious hours together. Nothing—do you hear me?' He heard her. He nodded. 'Now you go back to the car and wait for me there,' she instructed him. 'We'll discuss this intrusion of yours later.'

The first thing she did when she returned to the car about five minutes later was make a telephone call. As he drove, Shane could hear her side of the conversation. She was still clearly annoyed.

'All right, John, tell me what's happened, why the urgency? . . . Because I had something more important to do, that's why . . . Oh John, you know they're always doing that . . . every year when the contract comes up for renewal . . . you're panicking over nothing . . . they're always threatening not to sign unless the no-

strike clause is deleted, but they still sign nevertheless
. . . yes, I know, but they're always adamant . . . yes, I'm
just leaving the hospital now . . . he's much better . . . all
going well, he should be out of there in a couple of weeks
. . . yes, it is . . . now look, John, when I leave instructions with my chauffeur that I don't want to be disturbed, that's exactly what I mean, I don't wish to have
my orders countermanded . . . yes, all right, I'll see you
soon . . . goodbye.' She hung up.

'I'm sorry, Mrs Fielding,' Shane said quietly. 'I
shouldn't have come in.'

'All right,' she said impatiently. 'I don't like making
idle threats, but I'll let it go this time—on the condition
that you do not discuss anything you may have seen or
heard with any other Fielding employee. Do you
understand?'

'Yes, Mrs Fielding.'

'Good.' Shane heard the click of the lock as she opened
her attaché case. 'Now hurry. I've still got a lot of work to
do back at the office.'

The following morning, instead of having him drive her
to the office as usual, Mrs Fielding called Shane into the
house. She had some envelopes for him to deliver. She
handed them to him, then remembering something else
she wanted him to take, left him alone in the tastefully
furnished living room for a few moments while she went to
fetch it. While he waited, he looked around the room, at the
delicate antique furniture, the paintings on the walls.
Noticing a framed photograph on one of the cabinets, he
crossed the room to inspect it more closely. It was the same
man he had seen in the hospital room, but fuller in the face,
smiling, healthy. He heard Mrs Fielding's footsteps in the
hall and moved away from the photograph.

'Now I want you to take this to Mister Edmonds.' She
handed him another envelope. 'You're to give it to him
personally. To him—and no one else. And don't just
leave it on his desk.'

'Yes, Mrs Fielding.'

She gestured dismissively. 'Off you go then.'

'Yes, Mrs Fielding.'

As he was closing the front door behind him, he heard the telephone ringing inside the house. Disgruntled, he made his way back to the car. The way that woman talked to him . . . 'Yes, Mrs Fielding,' he muttered to himself. 'Yes, Mrs Fielding.' It was like a litany to be learnt off by heart.

Then, just as he was about to get into the car, he heard her calling his name behind him. It sounded urgent. He turned and watched her with curiosity as she ran towards him. She was clearly agitated. Something had happened. 'You must take me to the hospital,' she gasped. 'Immediately. My husband has just had a heart attack.' Without waiting for Shane to do it for her, she wrenched open the car door and flung herself onto the back seat. 'Hurry!' she cried desperately. 'For God's sake, hurry!'

She already had the door open by the time he screeched to a halt outside the front entrance to the hospital. 'Shall I wait here?' Shane called after her as she ran towards the steps.

'Yes, please.'

Worried, Shane watched her as she hurried up the steps. She had almost reached the top when a man in a white doctor's gown emerged from the building to meet her. They talked quietly together for some moments, and when Mrs Fielding tried to move past him to the door, he gently restrained her with a solemn shake of his head. She turned slowly away from him. She looked defeated—and Shane knew with something more than just instinct that they were too late. As if in a daze, she returned to the car. 'Please . . . Shane,' she said in a tired, dispirited voice. 'Take me home.'

Back at her house, Shane accompanied her inside. She looked so pale, so shaken that he didn't feel she should be left alone. In the hallway, he helped her off with her coat, then followed her into the living room. 'Is there anything I can get you?' he asked solicitously. 'A drink perhaps?'

She shook her head, and slumped into an armchair. 'I just can't believe he's gone,' she said distractedly.

'I'm very sorry.'

She looked so vulnerable sitting there, so young and so hurt. 'You know it will happen one day . . . but nothing prepares you for it.'

'I wish there was something I could do,' Shane said quietly, but he didn't think she heard him.

'Yesterday . . .' there were tears in her eyes . . . 'only yesterday we were sitting in his room . . . talking. He was improving . . . he really was getting better. They even said he could come . . . home.' The tears began to course down her smooth cheeks. The telephone rang. Shane moved quickly across the room to answer it. It was the office. He looked enquiringly at the quietly grieving woman who shook her head. 'No . . . no more . . . I can't.'

'I'm sorry,' Shane told the caller, 'but Mrs Fielding's not available at the moment.' He hung up. 'I think you should get some rest,' he suggested. 'I'll take care of everything.'

'Would you?' She looked up at him gratefully through her tears.

'Sure. Leave it to me.'

It was late when she emerged from her bedroom. Shane had just made himself a plate of sandwiches and cup of coffee. 'What time is it?' she asked drowsily.

'Nine-thirty,' he replied.

'Oh, I didn't realise it was so late,' she said in some consternation. 'You should have gone home.'

'That's okay. I had nothing else to do.'

'All the same . . .' She looked at him with an expression of concern. 'What about your family? Won't they be worried?'

'No.' Shane laughed softly. 'They're used to me keeping all hours.'

She sat down on the couch. While she was resting, the silence in the house had been quite oppressive. Shane had drawn the living-room curtains and switched on one of the floor lamps. 'I'm sorry. I didn't mean to leave you alone like this.'

Shane nodded to the plate of sandwiches he had just prepared for himself. 'I made myself some supper.' He picked up the plate and held it out to her. 'Here. You'd better have some yourself. You haven't eaten.'

'Thanks.' She took one of the sandwiches.

He made her some coffee and brought it back into the living room. 'Did you manage to get any sleep?'

'Not much.' She sipped her coffee. 'My mind just seemed to be going around and around.' Shane noticed that she had hardly touched the sandwiches.

'You must try not to think about it.' He knew it wasn't the most reassuring thing he could tell her, but it was the best he could do; he wasn't used to situations like this.

She had let her hair down. She was in her dressing gown. Her eyes were slightly puffy. 'I know,' she said weakly, 'but I can't help it. Every time I close my eyes I keep seeing his face.' Shane let her talk; he knew it would do her good to talk. 'He was a very kind man,' she said after a brief pause. 'Very considerate . . . very loving . . .'

There were tears in her eyes again. 'You don't need to talk if it upsets you,' Shane said gently.

'That's all right.' She managed a small, fleeting smile. 'I want to talk. I *need* to talk.' Shane waited while she gathered her thoughts. 'Those ten years were the happiest years of my life,' she said at last. 'I really loved that man . . . totally, without reservation.' She looked up at Shane. 'Do you know what they said when we married?' Shane shook his head. 'They said I married

31

him for his money.' She laughed briefly, bitterly. 'Not to my face, mind you. Oh no, they wouldn't dare do that. But I knew that that was what they were saying. Because he was much older than I was. Because he was rich. As if that mattered.' She stood up and moved across to the fireplace where she stood with her back to him, absorbed in her memories. 'He was going to retire soon. We had bought a place up north on the beach. We called it Shangri-La . . . corny, I know, but that's what it really would have meant for us. We wouldn't have grown old there . . . we would have had everything we wanted.' She turned back to face him, her eyes large and gleaming. 'Do you know the thing that really hurt . . . after all those years of working so hard? Her voice wavered; her lip was trembling a little . . . 'He never had a decent holiday. Tomorrow . . . he would have finished working for good. Tomorrow he would have been sixty . . .' her voice broke . . . 'Oh God . . . such a waste.' Then she seemed to rally a little. 'I know I've got to be strong,' she said with determination. 'Dan had so much courage. He wouldn't want to see me like this.' Her hands were clasped together in front of her. 'Even after the accident, he never gave up.'

'Accident?'

She nodded distantly. 'In the car. An eighteen-year-old youth, driving on the wrong side of the road. He had been drinking. He ran straight into us. All he got was a cut on the head. Dan was crippled for life.'

Shane thought of his own accident. A police chase. The fugitive car running straight through the red light at the intersection. 'That's terrible.'

'I talk too much,' she said with a sigh as she moved towards the doorway. 'You've probably got things to do. I'm going upstairs now to try and get some more sleep.' She gave him a bleak smile. 'You can let yourself out when you're ready.'

Shane took a step towards her. 'Is there anyone who

can stay with you?' he asked. 'Any friends?' She shook her head. 'It's a big house to be alone in.'

'I've never been alone,' she told him. 'Even after the accident . . . it always seemed that Dan was here, with me. Now . . .' she sighed again and shook her head . . . 'I don't really know.' She moved slowly through the doorway into the hall.

Staring after her, Shane was deeply touched. She had been through a hell of a lot. She shouldn't be alone in the house. He came to a decision. He would stay in the house with her tonight. After ringing home to say he wouldn't be back that night, he made himself as comfortable as he could on the couch, and eventually drifted into a fitful sleep.

The next thing he knew was that someone was touching him lightly on the shoulder. He rolled over onto his back and opened his eyes. Sunlight drifted around the edges of the drawn curtains. In her dressing gown, Mrs Fielding was staring down at him with an expression of faint surprise. She looked very wan and tired, and he guessed she hadn't slept much, if at all, during the night.

'What are you still doing here? I thought you would have gone home.

'I decided to stay,' he told her. 'I'm sorry if I've done the wrong thing.' Maybe he had done the wrong thing after all. Maybe he had been too presumptuous.

'No, it's all right,' she said with the shadow of a smile. 'I'm just surprised, that's all.'

He swung his stockinged feet from the couch onto the floor and sat up. 'Are you okay?'

'I'm okay.'

There was another reason he had wanted to stay in the house with her, something he wanted to say to her. 'I owe you an apology,' he said awkwardly. 'I guess that's one of the main reasons I stayed . . . so I could tell you.'

She was still watching him. 'Why do you owe me an apology?'

'It's hard to explain.' He ran his hands through his hair. 'For being so blind, I guess. For listening to other people.'

Her eyes showed a spark of comprehension. 'Oh, you mean . . . Superbitch?'

He nodded. That was what he meant—the things people had called her behind her back, while he had seen another side to her altogether. He had seen how vulnerable she really was. He had seen a woman in love. 'You know then?'

She laughed softly. 'I'm not stupid.'

'No, you're not,' he said fervently. '*I'm* the one who's stupid.' Very, very stupid for not having seen her for what she was.

'In many ways I deserved it,' she said a little sadly. 'My job was to run the business—not to have people like me.' Sadness tinged her smile. 'I think I succeeded on both counts.'

'Will you keep the business on?' Shane asked.

'No. That's one thing I did decide last night. I'm selling out. It means nothing to me now . . . without Dan.'

'What will you do?'

'What I should have done years ago. Move north. To the beach.'

'To Shangri-La?' It didn't sound corny to him at all.

'Yes.'

'What will you do there?'

'Go for walks . . . read . . . listen to music. Perhaps I'll do nothing at all.'

'Will I see you again?' Shane thought he already knew the answer to that question.

'Probably not.'

'You know something?'

'What?'

'I think your husband was a very lucky man.'

'Why?'

'Because he married someone like you.'

Three

Looking back on it, and with the benefit of hindsight, Paul Robinson realised it was when Gloria told his father that her own father was also an engineer that his attitude changed. 'Charlie Slater,' he had said with a frown. It was as if a penny had suddenly dropped.

Until then it had all been going along swimmingly. He had brought Gloria Slater home for dinner. She was meeting his family for the first time, and he was very proud of her. He was sure she would make a good impression.

And so she had. Everyone seemed to like her. Everyone was on their best behaviour, even little Lucy who hadn't been too happy at first at the thought of dressing up and watching her manners as she had firmly been instructed to do by her grandmother. The dinner was excellent; their grandmother had spent much time and effort in ensuring it would be just right. The conversation around the table was friendly and animated. Julie talked to Gloria about the bank where she worked, while Scott told her that he hadn't yet decided what he wanted to do when he left school, although what he really would like to do was travel north and become a beach bum—but as he didn't think his father would allow him to do that, he might as well go to university instead.

'Oh?' Gloria was interested. 'To do what?'

'I don't know, really,' Scott Robinson said with a shrug, while Paul smiled at Gloria to indicate to her that his younger brother was always like that, always

35

horsing around, making jokes 'One and a half engineers in the family is quite enough.'

Seeing that Gloria was understandably puzzled, Paul explained. 'My Dad's an engineer, and I was going to be one as well. I was halfway through my course when I decided to chuck it in and join the airline instead.' Where, of course, he had met Gloria.

'That's interesting,' Gloria said. 'That's one thing more we have in common. My father's an engineer, too.'

At the head of the table, Jim Robinson frowned. 'Charlie Slater,' he said flatly, looking as if a penny had suddenly dropped.

'Do you know him, Dad?' Paul asked his father.

'Oh . . .' There was the briefest of hesitations. 'I met him a few years ago. I wouldn't say I actually knew him.'

Paul didn't know why, but he sensed that Gloria was suddenly uneasy, but then he dismissed it; Gloria had nothing to be uneasy about. What he did notice, though, was that his father was more withdrawn than he had been before. But he dismissed that as well. He was so pleased that Gloria was making such a fine impression on everyone.

He told her so as he drove her home. 'I agree. Yes, it was a marvellous evening,' she said.

Paul was pleased. 'So you weren't bored to tears then?'

Gloria laughed. 'Of course I wasn't.'

After they had pulled up outside her house, he walked with her up the path to the front door where she hesitated. 'Well, good night,' she said, holding out her hand.

Paul looked at her. Was that all? He had already noticed that there were lights on in the house. 'Hey, fair's fair. I've introduced you to my folks. So why don't you introduce me to yours?'

In the dim light, she looked momentarily put out by this—but again, that could have been Paul's imagination. 'They're probably all in bed by now?' Was she hedging? Didn't she really want him to meet her folks?

'The lights are on.'

'They might have just left them on for me,' she pointed out as she reached into her bag and found her key. 'Just wait here a minute.' Fitting the key into the lock, she opened the door. 'I'll just go and check.'

Again, just for a moment, Paul was puzzled. It had seemed to him that her hesitation was brought about by a certain reluctance. But maybe not, he told himself. Maybe it had been brought about something else altogether—if there *was* a hesitation, and now he couldn't even be sure that there was. As he stood on the verandah, his hands in his pockets, waiting for her to return, he looked up at the house and the grounds in which it was standing. It was certainly impressive enough. A few moments later, the front door opened again, and there was Gloria, outlined in the light from the hallway behind her, smiling at him and beckoning him inside. Paul prepared himself to meet her folks; he knew how important first impressions could be.

His own first impressions of the room into which Gloria was now ushering him were of wealth and style. A fire was blazing cheerily in the open fireplace in front of which a man was standing with a glass in his hand. There was a half-full whisky decanter on the table beside him. He seemed very much at ease, unlike the woman who, also standing near the fire, looked on with an expression almost of apprehension as the two men shook hands. Gloria herself seemed a little nervous.

'Can I get you something?' Mrs Slater offered. 'Tea? Coffee?'

'Don't be ridiculous, Emily,' Gloria's father said in a slightly thickened voice. 'The man wants a drink.'

'No, thanks,' Paul said. 'I'm driving.'

Mr Slater's face was ruddy in the glow from the fire. 'Nonsense. 'One won't put you over the limit.' He picked the decanter from the table next to him. 'It happens to be a particularly fine Scotch.' He fixed his wife with a cold stare. 'Emily, get the man a glass,' he commanded.

'But Paul doesn't want a drink,' Gloria protested.

'Rubbish.' Mr Slater poured some more Scotch into his own glass. 'The boy's just being polite, that's all.' He turned back to Paul. 'So come on. Don't hold back. What will it be?'

To Paul it seemed he had no choice. The man was determined he should have a drink with him. He gave in. 'Oh, all right then. A light beer will do very nicely, thank you.' It wouldn't do him any harm, anyway.

'I'll get it for you,' Mrs Slater said, hurrying out of the room.

'It seems that you know my Dad,' Paul told Gloria's father. 'Jim Robinson.'

'Ah . . .' Mr Slater had just been raising the glass to his lips. Arresting the movement, he studied Paul more closely. In the fireplace, a smouldering log collapsed with a splutter and a small shower of sparks. 'Yes, I can see the resemblance.' He emptied his glass with one swig. 'Well, I'll be damned,' he said with a throaty chuckle. 'Jim Robinson's boy. The last time I saw him . . .' he thought for a moment . . . 'why he couldn't have been any older than you are now.'

Paul was surprised. 'I didn't think it was that long ago, Mister Slater.'

'Charlie, please.' Gloria's father gestured expansively. 'Call me Charlie.' He chuckled again. 'Jim Robinson, eh? You know, I've often wondered what happened to him.' He refilled his glass from the decanter. 'He's well, I take it?'

'Fighting fit.' Paul rather liked Gloria's father; he was certainly friendly enough.

'Any brothers? Sisters?'

'Two sisters and a brother.'

'Well, well, well.' Charlie Slater was shaking his head in mild amusement. 'Jim Robinson, father of four. I can hardly believe it.' He became quite confidential. 'I've always liked Jim, you know. One of the most honest men I've ever met.' He swallowed some more Scotch. 'Yes . . . ah . . . we should get together some time. I'd like that.'

Mrs Slater came back into the room with a can of light beer and a glass which, after a quick nervous glance at her husband, she handed to Paul. 'Thanks,' Paul said, then looked back at Charlie Slater. 'I'll mention that to him. I'm sure he'll think it's a good idea.'

But Jim Robinson didn't think that was a good idea at all when Paul suggested it to him. Puzzled by his lack of enthusiasm, Paul pressed him on the point. He had just come home from the Slaters'. His father was still up. The others had gone to bed. It was already after eleven.

'Look, Paul,' Jim said wearily, 'at the risk of being blunt, I didn't like the man then, and I don't see any reason why I should feel any different now.'

Charlie Slater had told Paul that he had always liked Jim Robinson. Now Jim Robinson was telling his son that he had never liked Charlie Slater. 'People can change, you know.'

Jim grimaced. 'Not the Charlie Slaters of this world.'

'And you won't even give it a try?'

Jim finished his coffee, and pushing his chair back from the kitchen table, stood up. 'All right, so you've taken a shine to his daughter. That's fine, that's okay by me. But that's got nothing to do with me—or anyone else.' Paul could tell his father was holding back his anger; he knew all the signs. But anger about what? Charlie Slater, who said he liked him so much, that Jim

39

was one of the most honest men he had ever met? 'If things start to get serious between you and this girl . . .'

'Gloria.' Paul was hurt by his father's cool dismissal of her after the evening had gone so well—or so he had thought. 'Her name's Gloria.'

'All right, I'm sorry,' Jim said woodenly. 'Gloria. If things *do* start getting serious, I trust you will let me know. But, until then it had nothing to do with anyone except you and . . . Gloria.' He moved across the kitchen to the door. 'Now I'm going to bed. I'll see you in the morning.'

After he had gone, Paul shook his head in bemusement. It was all very strange.

It wasn't until later that week, when Paul took Gloria out to dinner that he was able to bring up the strange attitude of his father towards Charlie Slater. He had brought her to one of the city's less ostentatious but nevertheless expensive restaurants—but that didn't matter, it was an occasion; Gloria was someone very special. He bought a single red rose from a flower seller who was circulating among the tables with a basket over her arm. Music throbbed seductively in the air.

'The last person to buy me a rose was my father,' Gloria mused. 'I nearly fell off my chair.'

'Why was that?'

'Buying flowers is . . . well, it's not his style at all. But there was a reason for it, I suppose. We were dining with clients of his at the time. I think they were impressed with the gesture.'

'I wouldn't have thought he needed to impress anyone,' Paul remarked. 'Anyone but you, that is.' He smiled at her across the table. 'I think you're very lucky, having a father like him.'

'You've got nothing to complain about,' Gloria said.

That was true. Paul had every reason to be proud of his father, but there were times . . . 'I'm a bit cheesed off with him at the moment.'

'Why's that?' The red rose was lying on the table in front of her.

'It's just the way he's behaving. It seems that there is some ill-feeling between him and your father.'

Gloria's smile faded just a fraction. 'These things tend to happen in the business world,' she said quickly, not looking at him.

Paul nodded. 'Yes, that's true—but Dad generally likes people, unless they've done something really bad to him. But as far as *your* Dad is concerned, he and my father have never done any business together as far as I know. So I can't see how that can be the case.'

'Does it matter?' Gloria was staring thoughtfully down at the rose. 'I mean, it needn't get in the way of our enjoying each other's company.'

'Of course not.' He leaned forward. He was still thinking of his father's reaction. 'Although I gather it's got something to do with professional jealousy. He just won't admit it, that's what I think.'

'Don't be stupid, Paul,' Gloria said with a sharpness that took him aback. 'Look,' she went on emphatically, 'all I know is that my Dad is no saint. So why don't you ask your father what it's all about before you start making judgements?'

She had a point, of course. Paul was feeling suddenly abashed. 'Yes, I suppose I should,' he said weakly.

Gloria sighed and shook her head. Then, looking up at him, she smiled. 'We've spent most of the night talking about our families,' she said, placing her hand on top of his own, while all around them the other diners talked, laughed, ate and drank, quite oblivious to this show of tenderness at the corner table. 'I thought the idea was for us to get to know each other better.'

Right, right and right again. That was exactly why they were here. That was why he had bought her a single red rose. He wished the waiter would hurry up with the dinner they had ordered. He was feeling ravenous.

Later, much later, after he had brought her back to her house and was walking with her up the path to the front door, both of them happy and joking with each other, Gloria carrying her red rose, Paul was startled to hear a muffled sobbing sound coming from the side of the house, then the rustle of bushes. Gloria heard it, too. They stopped on the path and stared at each other in alarm. Paul's first thought was that there was an intruder lurking in the grounds. But the sobbing . . .?

'What's that?' he whispered.

'I don't know.' Gloria's eyes in the gloom were wide and frightened.

Nervously, they moved off the path towards the side of the house where the sounds were coming from. They became more distinct as they neared the side path. Then Gloria said, angrily, 'Oh hell, not again', and hurried ahead. Puzzled, Paul followed her.

In the dim moonlight, as he rounded the side of the house he could make out a figure crouched on the path. Gloria was crouched beside it, had her arms around it, was comforting it. 'Oh Mum,' she was moaning softly, desperately. 'What has he done?'

Paul stood helplessly as Gloria helped her sobbing mother to her feet. He didn't know what he could do to help. 'He threw me out,' Mrs Slater gasped through her sobs. 'He . . . locked all the doors. I'd already gone to bed.'

Paul took a step forward. He couldn't just stand there and say nothing. 'Did Mister Slater do this to you?'

'Daddy dear gets very brave when he's loaded,' Gloria said savagely.

The woman was in great distress. 'I'll talk to him,' Paul said, cutting back across the lawn to the front door.

'Don't bother,' Gloria called after him. 'There's no reasoning with him when he's like this.'

'Just let me try.'

'Take us to a motel. We'll come back in the morning when he's settled down.'

Paul stopped and stared back at the girl who had become so special to him, and her stricken mother. He was feeling quite angry now. 'He can't lock you out of your own home. I *have* to talk to him, make him see reason.' He moved quickly up the front steps and rang the doorbell. He heard the sound of heavy, dragging footsteps in the hall, then a moment later, the door was wrenched open. Gloria and her mother remained in the shadows at the side of the house, away from the light that spilled out from the open door.

Charlie Slater was standing unsteadily in the doorway with a glass in one hand, his grey hair tousled, his tie loosened and his waistcoat unbuttoned. He blinked at Paul for a moment as he made an effort to focus. 'Robinson,' he exclaimed when he had managed to do so. 'My boy.' He grabbed Paul's arm. 'Come in. Come and have a drink.' He pulled Paul into the hall, then with his arm around his shoulder, led him through into the living. 'Damn women,' he muttered thickly. 'You share a house with them, but you can never have a drink with them.'

Charlie Slater had left the front door open. Paul gently disengaged himself from the heavy, clumsy embrace. 'I don't want a drink, Mister Slater,' he said. 'I think you've had enough, too.' He felt confident that he would be able to reason with the man.

'Mate, I'm just warming up,' Charlie Slater said with a laugh.

Paul was finding it difficult to keep himself calm and controlled. He was feeling quite disgusted. 'Mate, I've just seen your wife out the front,' he said in a clipped voice. 'She's freaking out.'

Charlie Slater was swaying slightly on his feet as he moved across to the whisky decanter on the sideboard and refilled his glass. 'Yeah . . . well,' he slurred, looking blearily up at Paul. 'Finders keepers, that's what I say.'

Paul faced him squarely. 'You could let her in for tonight at least. Then you can sort it all out in the morning.'

It seemed to be finally getting through to the man that he hadn't found a drinking companion after all. Now he was becoming antagonistic. He lurched back across the room to where Paul was standing. 'Listen here, Bozo,' he said, prodding Paul's chest with his finger. 'I threw the stupid cow out. Now why the hell would I want her back in?' His finger was still prodding. Paul stood his ground. 'You tell me.' He gave Paul a shove. 'Get out,' he ordered harshly. 'Go on, get out.'

Knowing it was pointless to argue any further with the man, Paul turned and headed back to the front door with Charlie Slater close on his heels. The front door slammed behind him as he stepped out onto the verandah.

Gloria and her mother were still waiting in the shadows. Paul felt very angry and frustrated. Perhaps he should have made a greater stand. He shouldn't have allowed himself to be shoved around. 'I'm sorry,' he murmured.

'Paul, if you don't mind . . .' Gloria's mother spoke quietly but still brokenly . . .' could you just take us to a motel.'

She was in her night clothes. Paul had a better idea. 'I think it would be better if you came home with me.'

Gloria still had her arm around her mother. 'I think Paul's right,' she said. She looked at Paul. 'Do you think they'd mind?'

'They won't mind,' Paul assured her. He began to move down the path. 'Now come on, let's get out of here.'

As they drove to the Robinson's house, Mrs Slater, huddled in the back seat with her daughter's arms around her, quietly began to sob again. 'You've got to leave him, Mum,' Gloria said flatly.

'I've tried . . .'

'But, Mum . . .'

'Gloria . . . please . . . I don't want to talk about it tonight.'

When they reached the house, Mrs Slater's main concern was the trouble she was causing. She was embarrassed at turning up like this so late at night, but Paul had insisted . . . She didn't want to cause them trouble. She and Gloria would go to a motel. But Paul's father and grandmother wouldn't hear of it. 'Don't be silly,' Helen Daniels said. 'You're staying here tonight, and that's final. Now come on, I'll take you to bed, then bring you a nice cup of tea.'

'Please don't think badly of my husband, Mrs Daniels,' Mrs Slater pleaded as Paul's grandmother led her out of the room. 'He was very drunk.'

Paul had offered to make the tea. His father followed him into the kitchen. 'He's an intelligent enough man,' Paul observed as they waited for the jug to boil. 'You'd think he would know what he's doing.'

'I doubt it.' Jim Robinson slowly shook his head. 'Anyway, the Charlie Slaters of this world don't seem to feel they need to justify their actions.' It seemed there was something on his mind. 'By the way, son, I'm sorry for the way I carried on the other night . . . about you and Gloria. It's just that it came as a bit of a shock, her being Charlie Slater's daughter.'

Paul looked at his father. 'Just what is it between you and him? he asked quietly.

Frowning, Jim thought for a moment. 'I may as well tell you,' he said at last. 'You see, Charlie and I were mates at University. He was a year or two ahead of me.' He smiled reminiscently. 'In those days I was full of

45

ambition, I wanted to be a world-beater. There's nothing unusual about that, of course. Every young man at that age has great plans. Well, anyway, in my final year, I came up with this idea, this plan for an inexpensive suspension bridge. It was unique. I didn't know what to do with it—so I took it to Charlie.'

Paul listened intently. The pattern was already beginning to form. The water began to boil, and he switched it off. 'He held onto it for about three months,' his father continued, 'then he gave it back to me. He said he couldn't understand why no one was interested in investing in it.'

'He was lying, of course.' Paul poured the boiling water into the teapot.

'I found out much later,' Jim Robinson said with a nod, 'that three of the major firms were clamouring for my plans. And Charlie . . . 'he laughed bitterly . . . 'good old Charlie sold them to the highest bidder.'

'Claiming the idea as his own,' Paul said thoughtfully. 'Yes, I can understand why you feel so bitter.' Good old Charlie had obviously done very well for himself.

'He was only twenty-five when he set up his own business,' Jim said. 'With the help of the money he made out of my plans. Those same plans would have given us independence, total security for the rest of our lives.' He gave his son a wry smile. 'I guess I was taking it out on Gloria. It wasn't fair, I know. I was reminded of what a fool I was. So, you can see . . .' he shrugged ruefully . . . 'we're not all perfect.'

'Dad, I never expected you to be.' Paul smiled back at him. 'Now I know you're not.'

Jim Robinson was still looking thoughtful. 'In some ways I guess I was just as selfish as Charlie Slater.'

'You just haven't been trying to justify your actions, that's all,' Paul pointed out.

'Just trying to enforce them, eh?'

'I've got to admit that I was a bit confused at first,' Paul said. 'I mean, most parents expect their kids to bring home people that are . . . well, all right. But one would think Gloria had an infectious disease the way you were carrying on.'

'No, it was only her father I had an aversion to.'

'And we could have been as wealthy as they are now,' Paul mused. It was tempting to think what might have been.

'That's true, but we could quite well have ended up in the same boat.'

The tea had brewed long enough. Paul began to pour it into the cups. 'What do you mean?'

'Do you believe in cause and effect? You know, getting out of life what you put into it?'

'Oh, Karma. Yes, I guess so.'

'So do I,' Jim said soberly. 'And that's what happened to Charlie Slater. So . . .' he smiled grimly at Paul . . .' that might be worth keeping in mind.'

Yes, Paul thought, it was well worth keeping in mind. Perhaps, in many ways, it was for the best that things had worked out the way they had.

Four

Julie Robinson was pleasantly surprised when, on his first day, the new bank manager called her into his office. She wasn't sure what she had been expecting—except that, surely, he wouldn't be quite so young and good looking. 'As you know,' he said when she was seated in front of the desk, 'running a bank is a team effort—and the better the team gets along the better the bank operates. That's why I like to get to know my fellow workers.' He smiled broadly. He was very friendly. Julie decided she liked him. 'My team mates.'

Julie began to relax. The summons to the manager's office had made her rather nervous. Without having even seen the man, she hadn't known what to expect—and now here was this dark haired, attractive individual smiling at her across his desk and talking about a team effort. 'You make it sound like some sort of sport,' she said.

He laughed. His name, she had learned, was Philip Martin. 'Well, I must say I have learned quite a deal about teamwork through sport. Naturally.' He spread his hands. 'Now that I'm down here, I'm hoping to see a lot of both.'

'The bank moves you around quite a lot, does it?' Julie asked.

'Yes, it does. But that's part of the job.'

She had noticed the photograph on his desk as soon as she entered the room—two children, a boy and girl, their heads close together, laughing happily at the camera. There had been no photographs on the desk when old Arnold was the manager. 'It must make it difficult for your family.' She nodded to the photograph. 'Are these your children?'

'Yes.' She could see the pride in his smile as he glanced at the photograph. 'The little terrors. Michael there is seven, and Debbie is nine.'

There was just the photograph of the children. There was none of his wife. 'Then the little girl's the same age as my sister,' Julie told him. 'Do they go to school locally?'

'No,' Philip Martin replied. 'They're with their mother in the country.' He quickly veered off the subject. 'Tell me about yourself, Julie. Do you live at home?'

'Yes. With my family. My father and my two brothers, my sister and my grandmother. My mother died.'

'Oh, I'm sorry to hear that.'

'It was a long time ago. My father and my grandmother brought us up. We all get along very well.' She amended this with a smile. 'Most of the time, anyway.'

'And what about interests?' he asked. 'Or do your duties here at Pacific leave you no time for outside interests?'

She was really warming to him. 'Well, I'm not one for . . . team sports,' she told him, 'but I do play tennis. I also read a lot.'

'What do you like to read?' He seemed genuinely interested.

She thought about this for a moment. 'Nothing really heavy,' she said. 'Actually, I prefer historical novels. I've read *Shogun* twice.'

'You're doing well just to pick up the damned thing,' he observed wrily. Julie laughed. Philip Martin settled back in his swivel chair. 'As much as I'd like to keep talking,' he said, 'I'm afraid I've still got a few more people to see.' He glanced down at a list on his desk.

'Marilyn Temple is the next one. Would you mind sending her in?'

'Of course not.' Julie stood up.

He smiled up at her. 'I've enjoyed our little talk.'

'Thank you.'

'If you ever have any problems, you know where to come.' He stood up. 'And Julie, it's nice to see some fellow romantics among us boring bankers.'

Julie was perfectly charmed. Yes, she was sure he was a romantic—even if he *was* married with two children called Debbie and Michael who were at present with their mother in the country.

That evening, as she was leaving the bank, she heard her name being called. She stopped and turned to see Philip Martin hurrying after her. 'Are you off home now?' he asked when he caught up with her.

She had planned to do some shopping first, she told him. She was getting the bus, she replied when he asked her if she was walking. Her own car was at the garage, being repaired. 'Then I'd be happy to give you a lift.'

'No, no,' she protested. 'That's very kind of you, but . . .'

'But I insist,' he said firmly. 'Now let's hear no more argument. It's not out of my way. It will be no trouble at all.'

With a quickened beat of her heart, Julie allowed herself to be conducted to the car park at the rear of the bank. It seemed that the new bank manager was taking an interest in her—and she was very pleased about that. More than pleased; she was quite thrilled. Particularly when he suggested that they might stop off and have a drink somewhere on the way.

It was the same the following evening. Again, he took her for a drink after work, then drove her home. In the mornings, before she went to work, she took even greater care with her appearance than was usual. When he asked her to help him choose a set of blinds for the

51

house he had just rented to replace the garish curtains which set his teeth on edge every time he looked at them, she was very flattered.

Of course, people would begin to notice sooner or later—but Julie didn't care. Let them think what they wanted to think—and even if Des Clarke did make the snide comment now and again, referring to the number of times Philip drove her home after work when she could quite easily be driving her own car, now that it had been fixed, that was hardly likely to make her pause and think of where it could all possibly lead. Not even when he reminded her that Philip Martin was a married man with two children.

'Des, Philip and I are just good friends,' she tartly informed him. 'And, anyway, it has nothing to do with you.' He should be more concerned about that stripper with whom he was sharing his house in Ramsay Street. It was bad enough that Julie had to work with him at the bank where he was the assistant manager.

'Friends?' Des snorted. 'Come off it, Julie. Don't give me that. If it was just friendship you wouldn't be pretending that your car is still in the garage just so you can spend more time with him.'

When Philip called her into his office later that morning, he was clearly ill-at-ease about something. 'Sit down, Julie,' he said, waving her to a chair. He moved around behind his desk, but didn't sit down. He regarded her with a small, worried frown. 'I'll come straight to the point. With his hands braced on the desk he leaned forward. Julie wondered why he was looking and sounding so concerned. 'People are talking about us.'

'Who?'

'The staff.'

Julie was sitting forward on the edge of the chair. The flowers she had picked from the garden that morning stood in a vase on the desk between them. A nice

52

homely touch, she had thought when she had put it there. 'What are they saying?'

'It's not so much a matter of *what* they're saying; it's what they're insinuating.'

Julie relaxed a little. 'Oh, that's just Marilyn and a few of the girls being silly.' Whispering together all the time, as if they had nothing better to do.

'Yes, but they do have a point, don't they?'

If they did, Julie didn't see it. 'We're not doing anything . . . wrong,' she protested. 'We've had drinks a couple of times. You've taken me home. Surely, there's nothing wrong with that.'

'All the same,' Philip said seriously, 'I think from now on it might be advisable if I didn't drive you home. You see, we're putting ourselves in an awkward situation.' He smiled tightly. 'I mean, it isn't as if I don't enjoy being with you. I do—very much. But I'm worried about your reputation.'

'I still say we're not doing anything wrong,' Julie said more sharply than she had intended. She was bitterly disappointed that he should be taking what was only idle gossip so seriously.

'Julie, you're making this very difficult for me.'

Unless, of course, there was another reason, she thought suddenly. 'Are you sure it's just that?' she asked him shrewdly.

'Well . . .' He gave her another smile, broader this time and a little wry. 'The fact is, Julie . . . I find you very attractive.' He moved around from behind the desk and stood in front of her. 'It's funny, isn't it? I've only just met you, and already I think I'm falling in love with you.' He shook his head. 'And I can't let that happen. I'm sorry.'

He was falling in love with her. That was the most wonderful thing Julie had ever heard. She felt a tightness in her throat, a faint stinging behind her eyes. 'Why?' she whispered. 'Why?'

'Because I'm still married to Loretta. And I'm trying to protect you.'

'But I don't *need* your protection,' she said shakily. 'What I want is . . . is that we should still see each other.'

'I don't think it can work, Julie.' He sounded a little sad.

'I was willing to take the risk.'

'That's it, isn't it?' Philip was shaking his head again. 'It's a very big risk. Too big. Even with a divorce my family situation will remain in a mess for quite some time afterwards. You know that and I know that.'

They hadn't talked much about his family. He had always shied clear of questions concerning his wife, in particular. 'I don't want to be with anyone else,' Julie murmured unhappily. She was beginning to feel sorry for herself. 'Ever since I was a little girl, people have made fun of me. But you don't. You take me seriously.' The tears welled in her eyes.

Philip stared down at her, undecided. Then, apparently having come to a decision, he said, 'Look, Julie . . . ah . . . are you willing to have dinner with me tomorrow night?'

Willing to take a risk? Any risk, no matter how great. 'Yes,' she whispered. The tears were coming more freely now.

'Here.' He handed her a handkerchief. She dabbed at her eyes with it. The letter 'P' had been embroidered in one corner of it.

As she left the manager's office, on the way back to her own desk, Des Clarke looked up from the papers on his desk. 'What did he want?' he asked, nodding briefly towards the closed door of Philip's office. 'Of is it too personal to repeat?'

She'd had quite enough of his snide remarks. 'Don't be childish, Des,' she snapped. Then she relented; there was something, after all, he might be able to do for her.

'By the way, do you think you can give me a lift home tonight?'

His smile was a little crooked. 'Why? Is your regular chauffeur unavailable?'

'Don't bother yourself,' she retorted, stung by his sarcasm. 'I'll get the bus.'

'No, no,' he said quickly. 'Don't do that. I'll take you.' He studied her seriously. 'I'm glad you've taken my advice and let things cool down a little.'

'We don't want any gossip, do we?' Julie said ironically. She placed her hand on the counter. She was still clutching Philip's handkerchief. Des, glancing down at it, noticed the letter 'P' which had been embroidered on it.

'What are you doing with his handkerchief?'

Julie had quite forgotten about the handkerchief. 'No, that's mine.'

'Are you sure? Are you sure "P" doesn't stand for Philip?'

'Positive, Des,' she said moving away from the counter towards her own desk. 'Absolutely positive.'

When Philip Martin called at the house for her the following evening to take her out for dinner, she introduced him to her grandmother and to her brother, Paul, who, until then had been chivvying her about the trouble she was taking over getting ready for her date. She had ignored him. She was very happy. She was sure that Philip had planned to take her to some place that was very grand and special.

When Helen Daniels asked him if he would like a drink, Philip shook his head, then looked apologetically at Julie. 'Actually, I'm expecting a rather important telephone call at home,' he said. 'So . . . if you don't mind . . . I've decided to cancel the restaurant and whip up something at home instead.'

'Oh.' Julie decided she didn't mind. 'No, of course not.' As she thought about it some more, she decided she would like that very much. There would be just the two of them.

She liked his apartment. It was small, but cosy, and she was pleased to see that he had taken her advice about the blinds. The telephone call he had been expecting came shortly after they arrived. After he had hung up, he fixed drinks for them both. He told her he would be cooking something in marsala. Julie felt very relaxed. She asked him about himself; there was still so much about him that she didn't know. 'And where will you go from here?'

He laughed. 'I've only just got here—and now you're trying to get rid of me.' Which was not what she had meant at all.

'You know what I mean.'

'Well, I would like to be where the big decisions are made,' he said. 'Head Office—that would be my ultimate goal.'

'You're the youngest manager we've ever had,' she told him.

'The youngest in the State,' he said proudly.

'And the most good looking.' She felt rather daring as she said it. She hoped it didn't sound too bold.

He laughed self-consciously. 'Well, I don't know about that.'

The meal was excellent. It was veal he had cooked in marsala. They drank red wine. When Julie told him it was much nicer, having a home-cooked meal like this instead of going to a restaurant, she meant it.

Afterwards, with the dishes neatly stacked in the dishwasher, there was coffee and brandy. Philip smiled at her. 'You know, this is the first time this place has actually felt like home. I suppose that's one of the drawbacks to this job—always being on the move. It's hard to make friends.'

'I hadn't thought of that,' Julie said.

Philip drank some of his brandy. 'People tend to take

friends and family for granted,' he mused. 'It's not until you're on your own that you realise just how important they are.'

'I suppose that's true.' Julie was suffused by a warm, spreading glow. It had been a marvellous evening. She didn't want it to finish. 'Well, at least you've made one friend,' she said, regarding him steadily, meaningfully. 'Me.'

'And a very nice one at that,' Philip said sincerely. 'But, perhaps . . . and I've been thinking about this quite a lot in the past few days . . . perhaps you should really be going out with people your own age.'

'No, Philip,' she protested. 'I'd much rather be with you.' She felt as if she had just made a very important commitment.

They drank more coffee, more brandy. Julie asked him if he missed his children. He told her he did—very much.

'And your wife? Do you miss her, too?'

'No.' He said it unequivocally.

'It can't always have been so bad.'

'No, it wasn't. In the beginning, of course, it was fine. The classic teenage romance . . . We were at school together. We couldn't wait to get married. It was the same year as I started at the bank.'

They were seated opposite each other, Julie in an armchair and Philip on the sofa. The single table lamp cast a soft, inviting glow. Rachmaninov pulsed seductively from the twin speakers. 'We were far too young,' Philip said reflectively. 'It was a mistake, of course. You see, she didn't have any interests or goals of her own—and she didn't seem interested in finding any. So . . . it wasn't long before she found herself unable to cope with my comparative success. The children, of course, provided some sort of focus—and if it wasn't for them we would have separated long ago.' He was silent for a moment. 'Looking back on it,' he

57

went on, 'I don't suppose you could say it was actually anybody's fault. It's just that I enjoyed my work, and she felt left out of it.'

It was sad, Julie thought, how some things just didn't work out, even though they had been undertaken with the greatest confidence and hope for the future. 'Wasn't there some way you could make her feel . . . well, included?'

'Oh, I tried,' Philip replied earnestly. 'Believe me, I tried. At least, I think I did. But when I took her out, to office functions . . . things like that . . . she would just proceed to drink herself under the table.' He sighed. Julie felt sorry for him. It must have been all terribly embarrassing for him. 'And there were other men. Once she even propositioned the boss himself.'

'Oh, Philip . . .'

'I was transferred very shortly after that.' He put his glass down on the table. 'Look, I'm sorry. I must be boring you with all this. Now . . .' he stood up . . . 'it's getting late. I should be getting you home.'

Julie stared up at him. She had already made up her mind what she wanted to do. 'I don't want to go home,' she said softly.

They stared at each other in the subdued light of the room. Julie experienced a tingle of anticipation that was at once delicious and a little frightening. Philip looked worried.

'Julie . . . I would like you to stay tonight . . . more than anything. And it's not because I'm lonely, or because I've never been in this situation before.' It was as if there was a tremendous struggle being waged inside him. 'But I'm concerned . . . deep down . . . that you're feeling sorry for me, and I don't want it to be like that.'

'Why would I feel sorry for you?' Julie was determined not to show her disappointment.

'Because you're that sort of girl,' he replied. 'And

how do you know I'm telling you the truth? I mean, I wouldn't be the first guy to spin some girl a story of marital woe.'

'Because I trust you,' Julie murmured.

'So there it is, you see. Now you'll understand why I can't let you stay.' Julie wasn't sure if she did, actually. 'I'm still married, he reminded her.

Julie felt small and foolish, 'I guess I've made a fool of myself she said unhappily.

'Please.' He took her hand. 'You mustn't think like that.'

Julie rose to her feet. 'I want to go home now,' she told him.

Her unhappiness continued throughout the following day, and the day after that. At the bank, Philip gave no sign to indicate that things were any different between them. He continued to drive her home after work.

It could only have been through Des Clarke that Julie's father learned that her new beau was a married man—and the measure of his concern was such that, suddenly, one afternoon, there he was, in the bank, saying he had an appointment to see the manager. Julie was dismayed. She had all sorts of forebodings. She was sure there would be an angry confrontation between the two men. She couldn't think of any other reason why her father would make an appointment to see the bank manager; he had never found it necessary before now.

They were in the office for more than twenty minutes. Julie kept glancing apprehensively at the door, wondering what was happening in there—indeed wondering if the two men hadn't already come to blows. And it would be over her. She was tense, very worried. But when they finally did emerge, they seemed friendly enough. They shook hands in the doorway. At least they hadn't come to blows, Julia thought—but that was hardly any consolation.

'What did my father want?' she asked Philip after her

father had gone. She had been still apprehensive as she knocked on his office and waited for his summons to enter.

'Oh, just a chat about his account.' Philip seemed rather offhand. 'That sort of thing.'

'What about us?' Julie insisted. 'Did he want to chat about us as well?'

'Yes, he did.' He gazed at her sombrely. 'He's worried about you, Julie. As any man would who loved his daughter.'

'He shouldn't have come here,' Julie said angrily.

'It was all right, Julie,' Philip told her. 'He did the right thing. It was all right.'

Julie didn't believe her father had done the right thing at all. The more she thought about it, the more angry she became. That evening, she tackled her father about what she regarded to be his unwonted interference.

'I'm concerned about what this could do to you,' he said.

'Oh come on, Dad,' she said tightly. 'I'm old enough. I know what I'm doing.'

'Yes,' he said, regarding her thoughtfully. 'You're old enough. But do you *really* know what you're doing?'

'You mean my notorious affair with a married man?' She tossed her head. She had just arrived back from work, and hadn't yet had time to change out of her uniform. 'It's my problem, Dad.'

'Yes,' he said. 'I agree.'

'And it's none of your business,' she snapped.

Jim sighed. He bore all the signs of a patient man. 'What you do has been my business for the past twenty years or so,' he said. 'It has become rather a habit.'

Even so . . . 'Dad, it's not what you're thinking. He's a very decent man.'

'I know. I've met him.'

'Then you have no need to worry.'

'He's married,' Jim Robinson said simply.

And that was the stumbling block. Her father couldn't see beyond the fact that Philip Martin was married. 'Yes, but not happily.'

That didn't seem to make any difference to her father whose own marriage, Julie knew, had been a very happy one right up to the time of her mother's death. 'He has a wife and two children,' Jim reminded her—as if she needed reminding. 'How do you think *they're* going to feel about this?'

Julie hadn't thought about this at all—she really hadn't. All she had thought about was Philip himself.

When, the following afternoon, Philip asked her if she would have dinner with him that night, there seemed to be something weighing on his mind. 'I need to talk to you,' he said. 'And if you haven't made any other plans . . .'

Julie hadn't made any other plans. 'Is there anything the matter?' she asked.

'We'll talk about that tonight,' he said. 'That's if you'll have dinner with me.'

'Of course I will.'

'Then I'll pick you up at, say, seven-thirty?'

'Fine.'

She was on her way out of his office when he softly called her back. Smiling into her eyes, he placed his hands on her shoulders and drew her close to him. He kissed her—and Julie knew that everything would be all right.

It was almost closing time as Julie emerged from the office. There was a woman waiting at the counter, youngish, well dressed and quite attractive. Julie hurried across to her. 'I'd like to see the manager,' the woman said pleasantly enough.

'We're just about to close,' Julie told her, 'and he's terribly busy. Do you have an appointment?'

'No, I don't.'

Julie looked at her doubtfully. 'Then perhaps tomorrow . . .'

'I'm sure he'll see me,' the woman said with smiling confidence.

'I can't promise anything,' Julie said with a glance at the closed door of Philip's office. 'What name shall I give?'

'Mrs Philip Martin.' The woman smiled sweetly. 'I'm his wife.'

Julie stared at her. His wife? She wasn't anything like the picture she had formed of the woman in her mind. She looked quite charming, quite sweet. Julie wondered if she really was quite as bad as Philip had made her out to be.

'Loretta?' Philip showed his dismay when Julie told him who was waiting outside to see him. 'She's here?'

'She said she'll wait,' Julie told him expressionlessly. It had been quite a shock for her to be thrust suddenly face to face with the wife of the man with whom she was quite sure she was in love.

'All right then.' He gave a resigned sigh. 'I'd better see her then.' He obviously wasn't looking forward to it.

As Julie ushered Loretta Martin into his office, Philip rose to his feet. 'Hello, darling,' Loretta exclaimed brightly, moving across to him with the obvious intention of kissing him.

'What can I do for you, Loretta?' he asked coldly.

'I'm sorry, darling.' She moved around behind the desk and placed a hand on his shoulder. 'I know you're very busy—and it's very naughty of me to turn up out of the blue like this. I promise you, I won't make a habit of it.'

He was clearly discomfited by her presence. Julie felt as if a heavy weight had suddenly lodged inside her. This woman, his wife . . . surely, he must have been painting a false picture of her. 'I've missed you,' she heard Loretta Martin saying as she closed the door. 'So have the children. They sent their love.'

'Who was she?' Des Clarke asked her as she moved numbly back to her desk.

'Mrs Martin.'

'His wife?' Julie guessed that he already had a shrewd idea who she was.

'Yes.' Julie nodded. 'She seems very nice.' Too nice to be the woman Philip had described. She felt weak, disillusioned, hurt and vulnerable. It had all been an act. She had made a terrible fool of herself. A complete and utter fool. She wanted to be alone.

After his wife had gone, Philip called Julie back into his office. 'Appearances can be deceptive,' he said after Julie had coldly observed that his wife wasn't anything like she had imagined. 'Look, Julie . . .' He stared into her eyes. 'We'll talk about this. I promise.'

'When? Tonight?'

'Ah . . . tonight. About tonight . . . I'm afraid I'll have to call it off.'

'Then you're having dinner with your wife.' Julie remarked bitterly. She felt totally excluded, small, and now somewhat grubby. Philip nodded. 'Philip, we need to talk about this.'

'I know that.'

'We can talk about it now.' She was becoming quite desperate. This was something that needed to be sorted out without delay.

'Julie, for God's sake . . .' He was plainly only just managing to keep himself under control. 'This is extremely complicated.'

'Later then.' She was clutching at any straw she could find. 'I'll come around to your flat afterwards. We can have coffee, and discuss it then.'

'It will have to be tomorrow,' Philip said firmly.

'Then she's staying the night, isn't she?'

'Julie, this is neither the time nor the place.'

'And everything you told me about her . . .' Stung by her disappointment, by what she felt was his deception, she was lashing out at him.

'There's no use becoming emotional about this,' Philip said unhappily.

Emotional! What the hell did he expect? After all the things he had told her. 'A marriage in name only,' she cried. 'And where will *you* be sleeping? On the couch?'

'Yes, I probably will.'

She had heard enough of this ridiculous charade. 'Why *lie* to me? all that talk about her being an alcoholic, halfway down Skid Row. My God!' She laughed harshly. 'She's so perfectly normal it's a joke.'

Philip held up a hand. 'This is going to take a couple of days,' he said deliberately. 'You'll just have to trust me.'

She had already trusted him enough. She had believed everything he told her. 'You've made a fool of me.' Her lip was quivering. The tears in her eyes blurred the outline of the man who was going to spend the night with his wife. 'I don't know what I did to deserve it, but you've made a fool of me.' She couldn't take any more. She swung back to the door and wrenched it open. 'I'm certainly learning the hard way.' it was true. She had been taken for a ride. It would never happen again—that was something she promised herself. Never again.

By the time Philip called her into his office the following afternoon, she had calmed down considerably, although she was still angry and resentful. 'Well,' she demanded acidly, 'did you have a cosy, domestic evening?'

'You've every right to be angry,' he said quietly. 'Don't you think it's been hard on me, too?'

Perhaps it was—Julie didn't know. 'Is she still here?'

'No. She's gone back.' He regarded her thoughtfully for a long moment. He didn't look very happy at all. 'That's what I wanted to discuss with you—you, me, my wife, the whole business.'

It had been a busy day in the bank, and Julie had welcomed that in the sense that it had enabled her to concentrate on something else other than Philip, herself, and his wife. She'd had a restless night; she had been in agonies—and today, wan, exhausted, she had set about her duties with grim determination not to give way to her unhappiness.

'Loretta did stay in my flat,' Philip told her. 'I went to a motel.'

Julie wondered why he bothered. Everything he told her now seemed to be so transparent. 'Do you expect me to believe that?'

'It happens to be true,' he replied with a touch of impatience. 'Look, Julie,' he went on. 'Loretta is actually two people—that's something you must understand. Perhaps you find that hard to believe, but that's how it is. That's how she's been able to cause so much trouble. After we went back to the flat, Loretta began drinking—as usual. We had a row—again as usual—and on this particular occasion she came at me with a knife.' He unbuttoned his shirt sleeve and pushed it back to reveal some sticking plaster on the fleshy part of his forearm. 'I can assure you it wasn't self-inflicted.' He lifted a corner of the plaster and showed her a portion of the thin laceration in his skin. He pressed it down again, then re-buttoned his shirt sleeve. 'So there you have it,' he said wrily. 'My happy family life.'

'But what happened?' Julie was shocked. She didn't doubt that what he had showed her was in fact a knife wound.

'She came down here to see a psychiatrist about her drinking problem,' he told her seriously. 'The appointment was yesterday, but she didn't keep it, of course. She refuses to believe that she's sick. She thinks she's perfectly normal—although deep down, I'm quite sure she's terrified. But she refuses to accept help from anyone. So . . . when she didn't turn up for the appointment, the doctor got in touch with me . . . and when I confronted her, one thing led to another, and this . . .' He touched his arm. 'Then she left. She said she was going home.'

'But what can you do?' Julie believed now that what he was telling her was the truth.

'I don't see there's much I *can* do,' he replied ruefully.

'I mean, about the children . . .'

He shook his head. 'She wouldn't hurt the kids.'

'I feel so stupid,' Julie murmured miserably.

'I'm just sorry you had to get involved,' Philip said gently.

And she had thought he had been deceiving her about his wife. She had virtually told him so. 'I'm sorry, Philip. For everything I said.' He took her in his arms. He held her tightly. 'I love you, Philip,' she whispered as his lips sought hers.

She had given Philip a photograph of herself. It wasn't a very good one, she felt—she was looking rather windswept, and she was squinting a little against the sunlight. But he had told her he liked it, and pleased, she had given it to him. He told her he'd had it framed. It looked marvellous, he said. He invited her to his flat for the dinner which had had to be postponed because of Loretta's sudden arrival. Julie had a better idea. Why shouldn't she take a few things to his flat and prepare the dinner herself? It was something she would very much like to do for him. After some hesitation, he agreed. He gave her the key to his flat.

'Do you think everything will be all right?' she asked.

'Of course it will.'

'It's just that I get a little scared at times.'

'So do I,' Philip said with a nod. 'So, I suspect, does everyone who is in love.'

In love. She was sure now that that was what she felt towards him. It could only be love. 'There are times when I think that nothing could stop us. Then there are other times when I think your wife could give us trouble.'

'But she can't,' Philip assured her. 'A year's separation is absolute grounds for a divorce. No, Julie, don't worry. Everything will be all right.'

Julie wished she could feel just as positive.

That evening, after she had gone home to change and do something special with her hair, she did some shopping. She bought the chicken which she had decided to roast, vegetables and a couple of bottles of wine, which, together with some flowers she had picked in the garden of her family's house she brought to Philip's apartment. Putting everything down in the hall, she found the key and unlocked the door of the apartment. She picked up everything again and entered the apartment, closing the door with her foot behind her. 'Well, well, well, if it isn't little Miss Innocent from the bank,' Loretta Martin said with a sneer.

To cover her confusion, Julie moved into the kitchen with her shopping which she placed on the table. 'I've decided to give you your picture back.' There was an edge to Loretta's voice. Julie flinched as something struck the wall near her head. There was the sound of shattering glass. Julie looked down at the picture of herself looking windswept, her eyes narrowed against the sun, which lay on the floor among the shards of glass and the broken frame. She forced herself to remain calm.

The woman had obviously been drinking. She was swaying on her feet. This wasn't the same woman whom she had thought so pleasant that day when she had come into the bank to see her husband—the one whom, foolishly, she had been prepared to give the benefit of the doubt. 'You're trying to take him away from me, aren't you?' Loretta Martin challenged.

'It isn't like that.'

'You brought him flowers.' Crossing to the table,

Loretta picked up the flowers and threw them at Julie, who ducked. 'You've no right to be in my house.'

'Loretta . . . please,' Julie pleaded. 'We can talk about it.'

Loretta snorted. 'That's what Philip always says. We'll talk about it. We'll sit down quietly and talk about it. We'll be adult and reasonable. But I don't *want* to be adult and reasonable.' The flowers lay on the floor near the shattered frame that had once held Julie's photograph. 'Not when my *family* is at stake,' Loretta cried shrilly.

'I'm not trying to . . .'

'He's mine,' Loretta screamed, launching herself at Julie, who, taken aback by the suddenness of the move, was not quick enough to scramble out of the way before Loretta's hands were closing around her throat. She gasped for breath, but Loretta's pressing fingers were blocking it. She struggled, but it was as if, in her despair, her fury, the woman were possessed with a strangth that was superhuman. Her face swam before Julie's eyes. Her own eyes were wild and staring; they were the eyes of a mad woman. 'He's *mine*—do you hear?'

Then, vaguely, through the rushing noise in her head, Julie was aware of other sounds. She heard quick footsteps, then Philip's voice as Loretta relaxed her grip on her throat.

'What the hell do you think you're doing?' Philip demanded angrily.

Julie's throat felt raw. Supporting herself against the table with one hand, she massaged her throat with the other. 'Julie, are you all right?' Julie nodded. Apart from a bad fright, no damage had been done.

'Julie was just leaving, darling,' Loretta said with an icy glance at Julie.

Philip took Loretta's arm. 'Come on, Loretta,' he said firmly. 'You're coming with me.'

'Where are we going?'

'Back to the clinic.' He turned to Julie. 'I could drop you off at home on the way.' He was still holding Loretta's arm.

Julie shook her head. 'No. I'll be all right.'

'I won't be long then,' he said, guiding Loretta to the door.

Still shaken, and not knowing how long he would be, she set about to prepare the dinner. She felt very sad at what had happened, very much alone.

He was gone for almost three hours. He looked very tired as he let himself into the apartment. The chicken was in the oven which Julie had set at a very low temperature.

'I didn't expect you would be still here,' he said as they embraced. 'Are you all right?'

She told him she was. 'Thank heavens you arrived when you did. I don't know what might have happened.'

'I know,' he said gravely. 'When she's in that condition, she just can't help herself.' He ran his hand tenderly down the side of her face. 'I would never have forgiven myself if she *had* hurt you.'

'Has she calmed down?'

'She's still at the clinic,' he replied. 'She was asleep when I left.'

'And the children?'

'They're fine. They're with a neighbour.' He studied her face searchingly, his eyes mirroring his concern. 'I'm sorry you were involved in all this. I can't let it go on like this.'

Julie was alarmed. What did he mean? That they didn't see any more of each other? 'Philip . . .'

'The thing that happened tonight,' he said worriedly. 'So far, *I'm* the only one who had been hurt by her. Now I can see she's not to be trusted near anyone she regards as a threat. Not even that. There are the kids,

69

and if she takes it in her head to hurt me through them . . .'

Julie was appalled. 'What will you do?'

'I'll see if the neighbours can keep them until I get them down here,' he answered slowly. 'I'll apply for custody, of course—make it legal. It shouldn't be too difficult, given Loretta's state of mind.' He held her arms. His face was only inches from her own.' Julie, you have to understand. I'll have to do everything to help her. She's a sick woman. Even though we're getting a divorce, I have to do everything possible to help her.'

'I understand that.' She understood perfectly. Philip was that kind of man. 'But you won't be alone. I'll do everything I can.'

He gave her a grateful smile. 'Julie, I don't think I could manage without you. And . . .' he seemed to be girding himself . . .' and when this is all over, I want you to marry me.' ⁓

It was exactly what Julie had been wanting to hear. 'Marry you?'

'If you'll have me.'

Of course, she would have him. She threw herself into his arms. Her happiness was complete.

When she told them at breakfast the following morning, both her father and grandmother were astonished.

'But isn't he still married?' her father asked doubtfully.

Julie was bubbling over with excitement. 'Yes. We're getting engaged.'

Jim Robinson looked anything but happy. Helen Daniels was at the stove, frying bacon and eggs in a pan. 'I see,' Jim said grimly. 'What has that man being saying to you?'

Julie was a little disappointed in his reaction to her ecstatic news. 'Dad, he loves me—and it's only a matter of time before his divorce comes through.'

'Julie.' Jim sighed as he regarded his daughter across

the table. 'I know you love him—anyone can see that—but have you really thought this thing through carefully?'

'Of course, I have.' She was beginning to be impatient. She knew her father did love her, and was worried by the thought that she might have her fingers burnt—but he didn't understand that with Philip, there was no way this would happen. He just didn't *know* Philip, that was all. 'It's what we both want.'

Jim was about to say something more, but Julie's grandmother forestalled him after giving him a warning look. 'It's just a bit sudden, darling, that's all.' The smell of frying bacon filled the room. 'But if it works out, and you're happy, that's what is important.'

Julie was grateful for the intercession. Her grandmother naturally understood more about these things than did her father. But then, her grandmother was a woman. She, too, had been in love, once. She knew what it was like. Julie looked enquiringly at her father who was buttering himself a slice of toast.

'Well, yes,' he said awkwardly, 'I do agree with your grandmother.'

Coming around the table, Julie kissed him. Then she kissed her grandmother. 'Thanks. Thanks, both of you. And if we can keep this our own little secret until I get things sorted out . . .'

'Sure, Jim said as Helen placed his breakfast on the table in front of him. 'Whatever you want.'

Her happiness remained with her throughout the day. She was dreamy, and smiled at everyone. She made plans. Oh yes, a church wedding, definitely. All her family and friends. Abstractedly, she doodled on a pad the outline of the dress she thought she would like to have designed for her wedding.

'Julie. I . . . ah . . . called in to see Loretta today.'

Julie tensed. Loretta. She was the only intrusive, jarring element. 'Oh. How is she?'

Philip had just fixed her drink. They were at his flat again. Tonight he had told her, it would be his turn to prepare the meal.

'We had quite a chat, about the divorce.'

'I suppose she made a scene,' Julie said.

'Actually, no. She just seemed to accept it. "Whatever you think"—that's what she said. She was quite sensible about it.'

Julie was tremendously relieved to hear it. 'Last night . . . when she attacked me . . . she seemed so possessive of you. I thought she might try to change your mind.'

'I think she realises now that there's no point in resisting the inevitable any longer.'

If that were only the truth. If Julie could feel just as confident as Philip about that. 'I hope so,' she said dubiously.

'I know it seems a bit of a mess at the moment,' Philip said, smiling at her. 'But it will be worth it in the end. Trust me.' Julie did trust him, unreservedly. 'Oh, that reminds me.' Philip reached into his jacket pocket and produced a small box. 'I was going to give it to you later, but I guess now is as good a time as any.' He held the box out to her.

With a quickening of her pulse, Julie opened the box. Inside, nestling on a bed of blue velvet, was a diamond ring. 'Oh, Philip . . .' It was beautiful. 'I didn't expect this . . . so soon.'

Philip took the ring from the box and slipped it on the third finger of her right hand. 'Do you like it?'

'Yes, of course,' she replied ecstatically. 'Now I'm officially engaged.'

He raised his glass. 'To the future Mrs Martin.'

She beamed at him over her own raised glass. 'To my future husband.'

'To us.'

'To us.'

When Philip came to the house to drive her to work the next morning he seemed very withdrawn. It was such a change from his mood the previous evening that Julie was concerned that something had happened that would affect them both. She was sure it had to do with Loretta. She was right. 'She's told the kids about the divorce,' Philip said glumly.

'But I thought she knew that *you* were the one who wanted to tell them.'

'Oh, she knew all right.'

'How did they take it?'

'I don't know. She won't let me see them.'

Julie felt for him. 'She can't do that.'

'She'll cause a scene if I try,' Philip said. 'And I can't put those kids through any more.'

'But, surely, she won't *turn* them against you. I mean, she won't be nasty about it . . . will she?'

'I certainly hope not,' Philip said without conviction.

Philip had told her that it didn't seem fair to present her with a ready made family, which would probably mean a lot of work for her. But that was what she wanted, she had insisted. All she ever wanted was a home of her own—and a family. 'You know when I'm with you like this,' Philip said tenderly, 'I just know that everything is going to be all right.'

They were in his flat, sitting close together on the sofa. They had just had dinner, and Julie felt quite drowsy and contented. The telephone rang. Philip swore softly. Julie sat back with her eyes closed, and waited for him to come back.

Then, hearing Philip's startled exclamation, she opened her eyes. Philip was just replacing the receiver. He turned and stared at her. His face was pale. He looked stricken. 'What is it?' she asked nervously.

'It's my little girl,' he said disbelievingly. 'Debbie. She tried to kill herself.'

She waited in the flat for him to return from the

73

hospital. She had told him she would be there when he returned, however long it took. She had fallen asleep on the couch. The sound of his key in the lock brought her to instant wakefulness. She sprang up from the couch. 'How is she?'

Philip looked drawn. 'I think she's going to make it,' he said listlessly.

'Thank goodness for that. Come and sit down. I'll get you a drink.'

'Thanks.'

'What happened?' she asked a few moments later as she handed him his drink.

'Loretta's sleeping tablets. She left them lying around. Debbie took some—enough to almost kill her.'

It was unbelievable. A girl that age . . . so young . . . wanting to do something like that. 'Surely, it must have been an accident.'

Philip solemnly shook his head. 'No. She meant to kill herself. When they flew her down to the hospital here . . . all she could say was, "I don't want to wake up, I don't want to ever wake up." And it's all my fault,' he groaned. Julie began to protest, but he silenced her with a look. 'I should have been there. I should have been there to explain to them about the divorce. I shouldn't have left it to Loretta.'

Julie was suddenly very still. 'Is that why she did it?'

'She's been blaming me for everything. Debbie's been taking it badly. He half-emptied his glass. He looked rumpled, very tired. It was already after midnight. 'I could kill her,' Philip said vehemently. 'She even said that I didn't . . . didn't care about them any more.'

It was just what Philip had hoped *wouldn't* happen. Julie recalled that he hadn't sounded very convinced at the time. 'Where was Loretta . . . when it happened?'

'In the next room,' Philip replied wearily. 'Drunk. Little Mike found Debbie asleep on the floor. He couldn't wake her up. He rang the neighbours.' Leaning forward, he ran his hands through his hair. 'She could have died.'

'Oh, Philip . . .' She sat down next to him. 'Do you want me to stay?'

He shook his head. 'I'm going back to the hospital. I'll run you home.'

'If there's anything I can do . . .'

'No . . . thanks.' He smiled at her wanly, and Julie felt so inadequate. 'I just want to be with my daughter.'

She was surprised to see him in the bank the following morning, but when she mentioned this to him, he told her that he was only in for a short while, some important documents that had to be signed, and then he was going back to the hospital. No, he said, there was no change in Debbie's condition.

'I'll come with you,' Julie said. Philip looked doubtful. 'I'll just wait outside. I don't mind waiting.'

'All right, then,' he said. 'And thanks.'

Standing beside his car, she waited for him outside the hospital. People came and went. She heard the rising wail of an ambulance siren. She had told Philip not to worry about her, to take his time. A taxi pulled up outside the hospital entrance and a woman stepped out onto the pavement. Julie recognised Loretta Martin. Loretta, looking very pale and shaken, saw her at the same time. She walked towards Julie, who turned away.

'Julie. I'd like to talk to you.'

Julie swung back to face her. 'There's nothing we have to say to each other.'

'I want you to leave us alone.'

'How many chances do you need?' The nerve of the woman, Julie thought angrily. 'You were left alone with Debbie—and she almost killed herself.'

Loretta drew herself up. In a strange ragged way she looked quite dignified. 'I know what I did,' she said

75

tightly, 'and I take full responsibility for it.' Her expression changed as she made an appeal to Julie. 'Philip and the children are my whole life. I love them. I don't want to lose them.'

'You already have.' Julie felt hard and relentless towards this woman who had made such a mess of things. 'Because you obviously don't care about them.'

'I *do* care,' Loretta returned defiantly. 'I care very much.'

'The drinking . . .'

'I didn't drink at first.' Loretta became more confiding. 'I was a frightened country girl with a successful husband. Drinking gave me the confidence I needed to cope.' She stared evenly at Julie. 'You've probably always had your family behind you. You've had the support you needed. I haven't. Now . . . Philip and the children—they're the only family I have now. I need them. I do care about them.'

Julie looked up at the looming grey façade of the hospital building. Somewhere in there, Philip was sitting beside his daughter's bed. 'I didn't take Philip away from you.'

'I know you didn't.'

'I love him,' Julie said, turning back to face the wife of the man she loved.

'I'm going to a clinic tomorrow.' Loretta looked frightened now, very insecure. 'And while I'm there, I need to know that my family will be supporting me.' Her fingers plucked nervously at Julie's arm. 'You have your family, Julie. Please give me a chance to have mine.'

She moved away towards the hospital entrance. Julie stared after her. The encounter had left her shaken and no longer sure of herself. The woman did need help. She did need all the support she could find. She thought hard. She came to a decision. She followed Loretta Martin into the hospital.

And it was when she saw them in the hospital room, Philip and Loretta sitting beside the bed in which their daughter was lying; when she heard Philip saying tenderly to the little girl, 'It's all right, darling, I'll be here, I'll always be here, everything will be all right'; it was when she saw that Loretta had her hand on Philip's shoulder, her other hand clasped over his, that Julie knew without any shadow of doubt that there was no room for her. With tears filling her eyes, she walked away. They hadn't seen her.

Five

Jim Robinson was a little concerned about the way the Sutton kid was using his brand new BMX bike which Bob Sutton had told him cost all of three hundred bucks. There he was, speeding up and down the street on it, making it rear up on its back wheel, slewing it around in tight circles—doing everything with it that it was possible to do on such a sophisticated and expensive bike. And what made it worse was the pride with which Bob Sutton watched his only son performing those fantastic tricks of his on the bike. 'Isn't that a bit dangerous?' Jim asked him.

The Suttons lived across the street. Young Bernie was their pride and joy. 'No, he's okay.' Bob Sutton grinned at Bernie, encouraging him to take even greater risks with it. 'He's just having a bit of fun.' He raised his voice. 'You're okay, kid,' he yelled to Bernie.

'You'd better get off the road, Bernie,' Jim called as the bike swooped towards them. 'I'll be bringing the car out in a minute.'

'He's all right.' There was a touch of defensiveness in Bob Sutton's voice. 'He knows what he's doing. I taught him myself.'

It wasn't long before Bernie and his bike were becoming a thorough nuisance. He swerved unnervingly close to people, he leapt it out from behind parked cars at oncoming motorists. It was as if his brand new bike had brought out an obnoxious streak in him. Then, on the day when he honestly believed for a few moments that he killed the kid, or at least seriously injured him, Jim Robinson decided he had had enough.

It had been one hell of a shock. One moment he had been driving along the street towards his house, then suddenly, he had caught a movement out of the corner of his eye, a blur which had abruptly materialised into the image of Bernie and his bike speeding towards him after turning out of a driveway. Jim slammed his foot on the brakes but it was too late. There was a sickening bump then a clatter as the three-hundred-dollar bike was thrown up onto the pavement. There was no sign of Bernie who had disappeared beneath the front of the car.

He was lying on the road near the offside front wheel of Jim's car. He was lying very still. Jim felt sick. He was sure the boy was dead. Rushing to his side, Jim called his name. The boy stirred. At least he was still alive.

'Don't try to move.' Jim knelt down beside him. There was no sign of blood.

'I'm okay, Mister Robinson.' Bernie's eyes were open, looking up at him. Jim breathed a huge sigh of relief. A little shakily, Bernie managed to retain his feet.

'Does it hurt anywhere?'

'I told you. I'll be okay.'

He looked as if there hadn't been much harm done. Jim's concern was dislodged by a wave of anger. 'Do you know what you almost did?' he grated.

'What do you mean?' The boy was watching him guardedly.

'You almost got yourself killed, that's what. You were riding on the wrong side of the road. Hasn't your father explained to you yet how to ride a bike properly?'

'Of course he did,' Bernie muttered.

'Then why were you riding straight towards me?'

'I'm sorry.' Bernie went across to where his bike was lying and, after giving it a cursory inspection to check that there was no real damage done, mounted it.

'Okay?' he called back over his shoulder as he rode off down the street.

It wasn't okay at all. He was furious. He determined to have a word with the boy's father.

Bob Sutton greeted him affably enough when he called at the house about an hour later. He invited Jim inside and offered him a beer, which Jim refused. He had just popped across, he said, to talk about the accident.

The Suttons had been watching television. Overriding Bernie's protests, his father had switched it off. 'Oh yes, Bernie told us about that.' Bob Sutton didn't seem unduly worried.

Nor was Jan, his wife. 'He was lucky,' she said.

'Very lucky,' Jim agreed. 'Listen, I've got some time over the week so why don't I spend it with Bernie? Teach him some of the rules of the road.'

Bob Sutton seemed amused by this. 'What do you mean?'

'Well, I was pretty shaken up by what happened,' Jim told him. 'Another couple of inches . . . Anything could have happened.'

'But what's that got to do with Bernie?' Bob Sutton seemed genuinely puzzled.

'It has *everything* to do with Bernie,' Jim said shortly. 'He was riding on the wrong side of the road for a start.'

'Now hold on there a minute, Jim.' Bob glanced quickly at his son who was sitting on the couch, sullenly witnessing this exchange. 'The way I heard it, it was your fault.'

'*My* fault?'

'That's right,' Bob Sutton said importantly, gesturing towards his son. 'Look, the kid's not hurt, and I'm perfectly happy to forget all about it. But don't blame him for the way you drive.'

This was amazing. Bob just couldn't see that his son might have been in the wrong. He didn't want to believe it, and it was Jim's job to convince him. 'It certainly *wasn't* my fault. Bernie was taking his life in his hands on that bike today, and to be perfectly frank with you, I think that if anybody is at fault, it's you. You should have taught him how to ride it properly before you let him loose on the street.'

'I taught him to ride it properly.' The tension was building up in the room as the two men grimly faced each other.

'How to balance, perhaps. But he sure as hell doesn't know the rules of the road.'

Bob Sutton turned to his son. 'Bernie, tell me again what happened.

Bernie glanced defiantly at Jim. 'I was riding on the side of the road. 'Mister Robinson came towards me.'

'And *I* was on the left side of the road,' Jim said. 'He was riding towards me. He was facing my car, Bob.'

'So what's wrong with that?' Bob Sutton demanded. 'At least he *saw* you were going to hit him.'

Jim felt he was fighting a losing battle with this man. Any battle that involved his son would be a losing one. 'The only reason I was going to hit him was because he was on the wrong side of the road.' He pointed to Bob. '*You* drive a car. *You* drive it on the left hand side of the road. So why on earth would you encourage your son to ride his on the right?'

Bob's anger was matching Jim's own. 'I'll encourage my son to do what *I* think is the right thing,' he snapped. 'And I told him it's safer to ride towards the oncoming traffic.'

Jim gaped at him in astonishment. 'I don't believe this.'

'You can believe what you want,' Bob said drily.

'And, anyway, I'm not the only kid to ride his bike on the right,' Bernie said resentfully.

'And they shouldn't be allowed on the road, either,' Jim told him, then swung back to his father. 'Do yourself a favour, Bob. Get hold of some books on road safety. Then, maybe, you'll see how you're risking Bernie's life.'

If Bob was about to offer some retort to this, Jim didn't wait to hear it. He had said what he had come to say—and he could see there was no point in arguing the matter any further. Not when Bob Sutton's mind was set the way it was in any matter that concerned his son.

The accident was still very much on Jim's mind as, during his lunch hour the following day, he collected some literature of road safety from the Department of Motor Transport. That evening, after work he took it across to the Suttons' house. Jan answered the door. Bob wasn't home yet, she informed him. She invited him inside. Bernie regarded him sourly.

'I've brought you something to read,' Jim said, holding the pamphlets out to him. 'Your father should read them, too.'

Jan was looking flustered. Jim guessed she wasn't having an easy time with Bernie. 'Honestly, Jim, there's no need for this.'

'I'll leave them, anyway.' As Bernie was showing no signs of taking the pamphlets, Jim placed them on the hall table. 'There now,' he said lightly. 'I've done my good deed for the day.'

But if Jim regarded what he had done as being a good deed, this view was not shared by Bob Sutton who saw it as anything but that. In fact, he regarded it as unmitigated interference. Furious, he brought the pamphlets back to Jim. 'Look,' he bellowed, 'I don't come barging into your house like some kind of blooming evangelist to lecture *your* kids.' He threw the pamphlets down onto the kitchen table. 'So don't you ever come back into mine.'

'Look, Bob . . .' Jim tried to keep it on an even keel. 'I was only trying to help.'

But Bob Sutton was obviously not prepared to see

reason. 'If I want my kid to read anything . . . anything at all, *I'll* decide what he should read—no one else.' He glared at Jim. 'And all this time, I had you pegged for a level-headed sort of bloke.'

The Robinsons were having their dinner when Bob Sutton had come storming in, red-faced and brandishing the pamphlets Jim had left in his house. Now Jim was only just managing to keep his own temper. 'Now just a moment, Bob,' he said tautly. 'In the first place, those pamphlets were just as much for you as for Bernie. In the second place, I'm sick and tired of parents not giving a damn about what their kids are doing.'

'Is that so?' Bob's face was flushed, his fists were clenched by his sides. 'So you're sick and tired, eh? Well, so am I. I'm sick and tired of people sticking their noses in where they're not wanted. I'm sick and tired of bloody interference in my family affairs.' He waved his finger in front of Jim's face. 'If you *do* have to stick your nose into other people's business, then do it with parents who don't care about their kids. I do care about mine. So don't go picking on me.'

'Bob.' Jim was still trying to make him see reason. 'I only did it as a friend.

'Well, you can stick your friendship.' He gestured angrily to the pamphlets that were strewn across the table. 'And you can stick your bloody books.' With that, he swung on his heel and stamped out of the house, the front door closing with a very definite sound behind him.

Jim shook his head in amazement. 'Can you believe that guy?'

The family had listened to the exchange in stunned silence. 'In all fairness, Dad,' Paul said quietly, 'you *do* come on a bit strong when you've got the bit between your teeth.'

Jim wheeled on him. Here was the attack being taken up from another quarter. 'Explain yourself.'

Paul looked steadily up at him. 'The kids at school

used to give us hell when we got our first bikes simply because you wouldn't let us out on the road until we knew all the rules.'

So? 'Ironic, isn't it?' Jim smiled grimly at his son. 'Here you are, criticising me for being obsessed with saving lives. And your very job with the airline depends on your being exactly the same with your passengers. So you tell me, Paul. What's the difference?'

And, of course, Paul was unable to tell him.

It was a Saturday afternoon about two weeks later, when they heard the news that there had been an accident on the main street. A young boy had been knocked off his bike by a truck. The boy had been killed instantly. It was Bernie Sutton. The whole street turned out for the funeral, and throughout the service Jim couldn't help but think that there but for the grace of God . . . It could have been Scott, or Lucy. It was sad that something like this had to happen to make one realise how much was taken for granted.

They had just returned from the funeral and were about to enter the house when Bob Sutton caught up with them. 'Can't stay long. I just came to thank you all for coming to the funeral.' Jim said nothing; there was nothing he felt he could say under the circumstances. 'There's something else.' Bob was looking unhappily at Jim. 'I owe you an apology.'

'Bob, there's no need . . .'

'But there is.' Bob's face was drawn and lined. He looked as if he had aged twenty years in the past few days. 'Every day of my life I'll regret not having listened to you. Because *I* thought it was safer for him to ride into the traffic, he's dead.' He shook his head woefully. His eyes were glistening. 'I killed him.'

Again Jim didn't know what to say. In a way, Bob was right. He would never stop punishing himself for what had happened. 'Lucy told me that the school's starting a training course . . .' He stopped himself. It was too late for Bernie. He felt so inadequate.

Bob was blinking back his tears. His voice was uneven. 'It's important to me that you know that I appreciate what you're trying to do . . . and that I recognise my own stupidity.' He took a couple of steps backward. 'I'd better go.'

'How's Jan?' Jim asked him.

'Making the best of it,' Bob said with a sigh. 'We'll get by, I guess. We'll have to.'

'If there's anything I can do . . .' Jim held out his hand.

'Thanks, Jim.' Bob said as they shook hands. 'You're a good man. I guess I really knew that all the time.'

Six

Max Ramsay had declared war. It was bad enough that he had this raging toothache, but since those new people had moved into the house next door he hadn't been able to get a wink's sleep at night. His nerves were stretched to their utmost; he was racked with pain—and now those bloody dogs.

They barked all night, and when Max, unable to take any more of it, yelled at them, they barked even louder. They were driving him stark raving mad. His toothache became steadily worse—but the trouble was, he refused to see a dentist about it, because if the truth be known—and he wasn't prepared to admit this to anybody—he was terrified of dentists.

'You've *got* to go to a dentist,' Shane urged him.

Max had been bellowing at the dogs again. It was after one o'clock in the morning. He glared at his son, and once again wondered if he had done the right thing by letting him move into the flat with him just because there was some trouble with his mother at home. 'All I need is peace and quiet.' He had taken aspirins and was holding a hot water bottle against his cheek, but the pain persisted.

'And a horse tranquilliser,' Shane observed drily.

Max gestured angrily towards the window beyond which the dogs were baying with wild abandon. 'It's his last chance. If those mangy mutts keep me awake tonight, then that means war—total war.' It was as if the dogs had heard him. They began to bark even more frantically.

But he couldn't sleep, no matter how hard he tried, how much he willed himself to sleep. As soon as the dogs fell silent and he was beginning to think that maybe now he had a chance, something would set them off again. At last, his head spinning, his tooth throbbing, he threw back the blankets in a fury and sprang out of the bed. As he rushed across to the window, he stubbed his toe against a table leg. He yelped with pain. It was the last straw. He threw open the window.

He yelled at the barking dogs. He cursed them and promised them an agonising demise—and again, the barking became more vigorous.

'What's going on?' Shane demanded drowsily. He had just been awakened by all the commotion.

'That's it,' Max groaned. 'I've had enough.'

'So have I.' Shane yawned. 'I'm thinking of moving out.'

'I'm a patient man,' Max cried. 'But enough is enough.'

'You're a patient man?' Shane looked at him quizzically.

'You keep your comments to yourself.' Grabbing his dressing gown, Max hurriedly donned it. Outside, the dogs were still barking furiously. 'My God, he'll rue the day he ever moved in here,' he shouted, then winced as there was a vicious stab of pain in his rear molar. He slammed the door behind him.

The house next door was in darkness, but with those dogs carrying on the way they were, it was hardly silent. Max pounded on the front door. 'Shut up!' he bellowed to the unseen dogs.

In the house, a light was switched on. The door was opened. 'Do you know what time it is?' an angry voice demanded.

Max glared at the tall figure silhouetted against the light in the hall behind him. 'Yeah, I do, and that's the bloody trouble. Do *you* know what time it is?' he countered, he thought rather effectively.

'It's three o'clock. In the morning,' the man in the doorway added unnecessarily.

'Congratulations,' Max said sarcastically, raising his voice to make himself heard above the sound of the dogs. 'So, if a dumb coot like you can tell the time . . .' his arm jabbed in the direction of the canine racket . . . 'why don't you teach it to them Hounds of the Baskervilles out there?'

'They're guard dogs,' the dog-owner replied curtly. 'They're *supposed* to bark.'

'They're doing a great job, mate,' Max retorted. He peered at the other man. A fleshy face, receding hair. 'How do you manage to sleep at night? Are you deaf, or something?'

'I think you're exaggerating.'

'I'm not, mate. Listen, It's keeping the whole neighbourhood awake,' Max said, although there was no evidence of it, no lights being switched on, no angry yells to the dogs to shut up. 'What is this place, anyway, that you've got to have guard dogs barking all the time? Fort Knox?'

'That's no business of yours.'

'It will be, if you don't do something about those mongrels.'

'Well, you know what you can do.' The man was about to slam the door in his face. Max stopped it with his foot.

'I'm warning you,' he shouted. 'You either keep those animals quiet—muzzle them, poison them, whatever—or I'll report them to the Council. I'll say they've got rabies.'

'Rabies.' The man in the doorway laughed drily. 'Sure.'

'I'll get the cops onto you,' Max promised. 'I'll get a petition going in the street. I . . .' his anger was almost choking him . . . 'I'm warning you.'

89

'I've already told you what you can do,' the man said, and this time did manage to slam the door in his face.

With his tooth throbbing, his toe still hurting, Max limped back down the path to the accompaniment of the canine chorus. If that was the way it was going to be, he thought savagely, then that was the way it was going to be. As long as those dogs kept barking their stupid heads off, there was no way he would allow the matter to rest.

Later that morning, he had an idea. He telephoned his house, and when Marie answered, asked to speak to Danny—but Danny had already left for school. 'It must be the first time he's ever left early for school,' Max said ungraciously.

'What's the matter?'

'Nothing. I just wanted him to do me a favour.'

'Shane was telling me about your tooth,' Marie said. 'How long as it been playing up this time?'

'That Shane,' Max muttered. 'He's got a big mouth.'

'I wonder where he gets it from,' his estranged wife said acidly. Max hung up in disgust.

Shane had already been out for a jog. 'Ah, bright as a button again this morning, aren't we?' he said as his father re-entered the flat.

Max was in no mood for idle banter. 'You told your mother about my toothache,' he accused.

'Well, it's the truth, isn't it?'

'That still isn't any reason to tell her.'

'You need to see a dentist.'

'All I need is some peace and quiet,' Max returned. 'And rest from those bloody dogs—*and* from your mother's nagging.'

'Get some ear plugs,' Shane suggested brightly.

'No way.' Max shook his head. 'I'm going to play that guy next door at his own game.'

'How?'

And that was where Danny's tape recorder came in. But as Max and Danny waited with the tape recorder in the alleyway behind the house next door, there was not a sound out of the dogs. Max was furious. Just when he wanted them to bark, they had suddenly dried up. It was as if they had sensed his purpose. Danny was becoming impatient. It was his half day off from school, and the one thing he hadn't anticipated doing with his free time was lurking in a alleyway with a tape recorder waiting for dogs to bark.

'Why can't we just dub in some dog sounds?' he suggested.

'And how do you suppose we should do that?'

'I don't know,' Danny shrugged.

'They have to be *his* dogs.' Max nodded to the fence behind which the dogs were being obstinately quiet.

'But we've been here for ages,' Danny pointed out, 'and they haven't barked yet.'

Not a peep, Max thought in disgust. 'They're probably sleeping. They spent all the night barking. They have to sleep some time. Come here.' With Danny reluctantly following him, he moved around to the side of the house and stopped beside a barred window. 'Go on, make some cat noises, stir them up.'

Danny refused. 'If you want the dogs to bark, *you* make the cat noises.'

Max gave him a fierce look, then moved closer to the fence. Embarrassed now, he looked around him, then tentatively, made a harsh mewing sound which he *thought* sounded like a cat. Nothing happened. He tried again—then again. Obviously trying to keep a straight face, but without much success, Danny was squatting beside the tape recorder, ready to press the record button as soon as the dogs started to bark, which they were resolutely refusing to do. Max mewed again. A desultory bark came from the other side of the fence. Encouraged, and with a signal to Danny at the tape recorder, Max continued to mew. The barking became more intense. Max was triumphant. At last, at long last, he was getting exactly what he wanted. Very soon now, his revenge would be complete.

Later that day, he hired a couple of speakers which he had set up against the open window, facing outward, where they would produce the maximum effect. He could hardly wait to set them in action. He waited in gleeful anticipation for the dogs to begin their nightly racket. When they did begin to bark, at about midnight, he joyfully rubbed his hands together. 'That's it,' he cried encouragingly through the window. 'Come on, keep it up, you can do better than that.'

He was still awaiting his moment when Shane returned to the flat. 'Where did you get the speakers?' he wanted to know.

'I hired them.' Max's finger was hovering over the play button of Danny tape recoder.

'What for?'

'If I can't get any sleep,' Max happily promised him, 'then neither will anyone else.'

'Dad, please. This is getting out of hand.'

It was only just beginning. Those dogs were making beautiful music out there. Max chuckled. 'This will settle his Meaty Bites. Come on, come *on*.'

'Dad, it's nearly midnight.'

'I know what the time is. Now . . .' Max studied his wristwatch. The countdown was about to begin. 'Three . . . two . . . one . . . *zero*!' His finger pressed down on the button—and immediately the greatly magnified sound of barking dogs blasted out into the night. The room reverberated with it. Max had never heard such a magnificent, heroic sound. Shane clapped his hands over his ears, then dived for the recorder to switch it off. Max stopped him. 'Leave it alone,' he commanded. 'It's my revenge.' And how sweet it was. The hounds of hell baying into the night. A whole army of dogs.

'You're mad,' Shane shouted above the din. 'They'll put us in gaol.'

Max was jealously guarding his machine from further onslaught. He pointed to the window, 'Yeah, and *he'll* go with me.'

Then there was another voice yelling at him, this time from outside. 'What the hell's going on up there?'

Max rushed across to the window and leaned out. Yes, there he was, the neighbour, in his dressing gown. 'Ask not for whom the dogs bark, mate,' Max bellowed down at him.' They bark for *you* . . . blockhead.' He laughed. He was thoroughly enjoying himself. Catching a movement out of the corner of his eye, he turned to see that Shane was making for tape recorder again. 'Get out of there,' he cried, blocking him. 'It's mine, Shane. This is for me.' He clapped his hands together. 'Come on, you beauties,' he shouted exultantly as the noise drove in around him from all sides.

'Cut it out, Dad.' Shane was still trying to reach the recorder. 'He's got the message.'

But the dogs hadn't. They were still barking. 'What do you expect him to do at this hour?' Shane demanded. 'Shoot them?'

'That's not a bad idea.' Suddenly, there was a violent pounding at the door. 'Aha, action at last.' As Max moved to the door, Shane turned off the machine. The neighbour's barking dogs sounded almost quiet after that. The neighbour himself was standing at the door. 'Greetings,' Max said affably. 'Does your old heart good, doesn't it, to hear a couple of happily barking dogs?'

'Are you crazy?' The neighbour looked very angry. His face was white and strained.

'I'm pretty close to it,' Max replied, 'thanks to your flaming animals.' He waved his finger threateningly in front of the other man's nose. 'Look, mate, I'm going to report those dogs of yours. If they're not quiet tomorrow night, then you'll be getting more noise from mine until they are.'

'You'll be hearing from my solicitor about this.'

'Why not?' Max said. 'I'd just love to see you in court.'

The neighbour glared at Max murderously, then, turning, headed purposefully off back down the passage. Feeling quite pleased with himself. 'Good one, Dad,' Shane said ironically.

'He backed down.' Max was jubilant. 'Did you see that? I won. I proved my point.'

'I wouldn't bet on it, Dad,' Shane remarked wryly. 'I wouldn't bet on that at all.'

Max was still full of cheer as he and Shane sat down to breakfast. It was, he said, a wonderful morning. A new day dawning, peace and quiet in the offing. He bit into a slice of toast, then gave a cry of pain as it came in contact with the exposed nerve of his decaying tooth. Shane stood up. 'Right, that's it, Dad,' he said adamantly. 'No more putting it off. You're going to see the dentist, even if I have to chain you to the chair.'

The pain was excruciating. 'Shane . . .'

'I'm making an appointment for you, right now.' Shane headed for the door.

Max was in too much pain to argue. In his exasperation, he picked up an orange from the bowl on the table and flung it at the door which was just closing behind Shane.

The pain still hadn't abated when, about an hour later, Shane led him into the dentist's waiting room, Max was petrified, and on the way across had been tempted to give in to the impulse to make a dash for it, and to hell with the pain, he would just have to learn to live with it. But Shane had kept a watchful eye on him. Shane was determined to see this thing through, which was all right for him because he didn't have to undergo the agonies Max knew would be his lot once they had him helplessly pinned down in the dentist's chair.

'Come on, Dad. The worst is over. You're here now.'

The worst was about to begin. Max's tooth throbbed. A girl in a nurse's uniform said, 'Doctor will see you now', and Max wondered if it still wasn't too late to turn and run.

And then, there was the man himself in his surgery in a white coat, slowly turning from the basin where he had been washing his hands . . . and Max gaped at him. A fleshy face, receding hair and a dawning smile that was altogether too sadistic. Max could feel his knees buckling beneath him. A dentist, a neighbour, and . . . oh, my God, a dog-lover.

Seven

Danny wasn't impressed. No sooner had his parents decided to get a divorce than his mother was flitting around, getting all excited just because that insurance assessor guy was taking her out to dinner, which was some big deal. His name was Richard Morrison, and Danny didn't like him. He thought his mother was doing the wrong thing.

If it hadn't been for the robbery there would have been no Richard Morrison. Danny remembered the chaos that night, after he had taken his mother out to dinner and a show, and they had returned to find the house an absolute shambles. Then Richard Morrison had turned up to make an assessment of the loss, and the next thing Danny knew was that he was taking his mother out to dinner.

Now that Shane had gone to live with their father in the flat he had been renting since leaving home, Danny felt particularly responsible towards his mother. He didn't bother to hide his hostility towards the man he regarded as an interloper, which, though now divided, was still a family nevertheless, with every possibility, he hoped sincerely, of being one again in fact as well as in name.

Seething with impatience, he waited up, toying with his homework, but hardly concentrating on it, because his mind was too full of other things. Finally, he heard the front door close, then footsteps in the hall. 'Where have you been?' he demanded petulantly, without looking up from his homework.

But it wasn't his mother. It was Shane. 'Sorry,' Danny muttered when he realised this. 'I thought you were somebody else.'

'No one else lives here but Mum,' Shane reminded him.

'And even she's out for most of the night,' Danny said in disgust. When Richard Morrison had called for her, he had been full of sleazy charm. He had tried to make friends with Danny while waiting for Danny's mother to get ready, but Danny had seen right through him—and God only knew what was happening right at this very moment.

'What's going on, squirt?'

Danny told him. 'Mum's fallen for this guy like a ton of bricks. Some insurance salesman.'

'Oh yes. Dad said something about an insurance guy. He didn't like him, either.'

'Max is right.'

Shane was leaning against the door frame with his arms folded. He looked at his younger brother in surprise. 'This guy really must have got to you if you're agreeing with Dad.'

'Well, if Mum likes him . . .'

'I think you're over-reacting,' Shane said. 'Dad, too. She can't spend the rest of her life just pleasing us. It's time she started thinking of herself.'

Danny was stung. 'It's okay for you, isn't it?' he returned sharply. 'You don't live here. You don't have to put up with the guy. I do.'

Shane shrugged. 'Until I meet him, I'm not making a decision either way.' He straightened from the door frame. 'Look, Danny,' he said a little tersely, 'you'd better wake up to yourself. Because if it comes to a point where Mum has to make a decision between you and this guy, then I think I know which one she'll make.'

And that was the trouble, Danny had to admit to himself after Shane had gone; that was what frightened him. He knew, too, what decision she would make if it came to the crunch—and in her vulnerable state, with a divorce looming and all the rest of it, she was a woman who could easily find herself falling in love, and that would be terrible.

Things were happening too fast. The next thing she was telling him was that she was thinking of going away for the weekend. Danny's heart sank. 'Where to?' he asked glumly. He knew what weekends away could entail—motel rooms and self-conscious smiles at the breakfast table, long walks and meaningful discussions about the future. Danny had read about that sort of thing.

She had been looking quiet radiant when she arrived back home. Now, bringing up this business about the weekend, she seemed rather ill-at-ease.

'To the beach,' she replied. 'I could do with the break.'

'Where will you be staying?'

'A friend's house.'

'What friend?' Did he really need to ask?

'Richard.'

'I thought so.' He gave his mother a contemptuous look. 'You're pathetic—did you know that?' he cried bitterly as he stormed out of the room. 'Really pathetic.'

She followed him to his room. 'Danny, are you trying to provoke me?' Danny shrugged. 'I want to know what the matter is with you.'

'What do you want to hear?' There was so much bottled up inside him. He tried to sound offhand.

'The truth.'

'Yours . . . or mine?'

'Danny, I know what I see and feel.' She was on the defensive. Danny kept his back turned to her. 'I feel guilty, if you really must know—perhaps more. I feel angry and resentful at the way you are behaving. And I don't want . . .' Danny knew she was trying to reach out to him, was pleading for his understanding . . . 'I don't want to feel that way about you. It hurts.'

Danny wished that it could be different. 'Why do you always blame me for everything?'

'Listen to me, Danny. *Look* at me.' Slowly, Danny turned to face her. She had made herself up nicely for her evening out. She was wearing one of her best dresses. He could smell her perfume. 'Richard and I are just friends,' she said.

'He's all over you like a rash.' Danny's tone was cutting.

'I'm not going to beg, Danny.'

Danny shook his head. 'You don't have to beg, Mum. And, anyway, while you're away on this weekend of yours, I'll have be having a good time.'

'How?' A faint concern appeared in her eyes, just as Danny had intended it should do. 'What will you be doing?'

'I'm going to a party,' he told her airily. He knew she worried about him at parties. 'But you needn't worry. I can look after myself.' A twist of the knife. 'I've been doing a lot of that lately.'

'Danny, that's not fair.'

'And neither is what is happening to this family,' Danny said coldly.

Danny wasn't surprised that his mother should have discussed the problem with Helen Daniels next door. Helen was an older woman, she was quite wise. Maria Ramsay and she were great friends; Marie confided all her problems to her.

Danny was returning from the local shop with a carton of milk his mother had sent him to buy. Helen Daniels was sweeping up leaves on her front lawn. 'Good morning, Mrs Daniels,' Danny greeted her.

'Danny.' Helen Daniels stopped sweeping the leaves. Arrested by her commanding tone, Danny turned back. She stood with the rake in her hand, regarding him stonily. 'Have you any idea how much you've upset your mother?'

'I haven't done anything,' Danny protested, secretly pleased to hear that he had managed to upset his mother.

Helen Daniels spoke reproachfully. 'She deserves the best life can offer her, and Richard Morrison could have given it to her. Now she may never see him again.'

'That's nothing to do with me.' If it was true, and she *wasn't* going to see him again . . . That was what she would have told Helen Daniels. She would have been very unhappy about it, of course—but, Danny knew in his own mind, and with a strong sense of relief, that it would be for the best. 'I'm only trying to protect her, Mrs Daniels.'

'You don't appreciate what she's done for you.'

'Of course I do.' He appreciated everything his mother had done for him, for the family. Surely, what he was doing now was in acknowledgment of that.

But it seemed that Mrs Daniels didn't see it in the same light. 'Then you should be encouraging her,' she said tartly, 'and not behaving like a spoilt brat.'

But it wasn't working out as Danny had hoped it would. If one weekend was cancelled, there were still other weekends. His mother could still invite this Richard Morrison home for dinner. Danny was dismayed when she told him this. He had honestly believed that she had seen some sense at last, had had a quiet and regretful word with him, had realised, no matter how painfully, that her family did come first after all. But no . . . And not only that, but she had suggested, oh so nicely, that he might make himself scarce while Richard was there. Perhaps he could go next door, to the Robinsons, sit with Scott . . . but she really would like to be alone with Richard. She wanted it to be a pleasant, harmonious evening. She had given him ten dollars so that he could go to the movies, and that was rubbing salt into the wound.

'You haven't met him,' he complained that afternoon to Scott Robinson who was trying to do his homework. 'He's a creep. I tell you, he's weird. I mean, the way Mum has changed since he came on the scene. She's become really hard.'

Scott looked up from his homework. 'Come on,' he said disbelievingly. 'There's no way she'd kick you out for the evening.'

'Oh no? Then why did she offer me ten bucks? She said she wanted peace and quiet.' Becoming more agitated, he paced restlessly up and down the Robinson living room. 'I mean, I live there—and she's throwing me out. I get the bird—and he gets the chicken casserole.'

Scott was frowning down at the papers spread out on the table in front of him. 'Look, Scott, do you mind? I've got to do this homework, so why don't you come back later? Have dinner with us. I'll tell Gran so that she can put on a little extra.'

'Thanks.' Danny sat down. 'You know what really gets me about this?' he went in the same aggrieved tone. It was doing him good to let off steam, even if Scott was proving a reluctant listener. 'It's the fact that Mum and Dad are not even divorced. Mum's still married—and here she is, seeing another guy.'

'Perhaps she's lonely,' Scott suggested.

Danny wouldn't hear of it. 'She's got heaps of friends. A lot more than the old man—and *he* doesn't have a woman on the go.'

'Does he know about this guy?' Scott asked.

'I don't think so,' Danny replied. He thought of something. 'Hey, maybe if he did, he would do something about it. I mean, all this divorce business—it's crazy.'

Scott was regarding him quizzically. 'I thought you

were glad when they split up. Don't tell me you want them back again?'

Sure, Max had done all the shouting and abusing around the place when he was living there—but he had his good points, one or two of them. But more than that, for good or for worse, he was *family*. Richard Morrison wasn't. He was an interloper, a home-breaker. He had made Danny's mother turn hard. 'I'd rather have Max for a father than Morrison,' he stated simply. 'Yes.' He stood up. He had made up his mind. He would see Max and find out *he* felt about this whole sorry business.

Max regarded his son with some suspicion when Danny turned up at his small, cramped and untidy flat and began to talk about nothing in particular.

'All right then, what is it?' he demanded gruffly. 'What's happened? I can't believe you've come here to find out my state of health.'

Danny looked at him innoncently. 'Do I need an excuse to visit you?'

'You don't.' Max shook his head. 'Just tell me the truth when you get here, that's all.' He stared at Danny closely. 'You and your mother have had a blue, haven't you?'

'Not much of one,' Danny said with a shrug.

'And how much of a blue is that?'

'About ten dollars worth.'

'Come on, Danny. Out with it.'

'Well . . .' Danny tried to make it sound convincing; whatever else he was, he knew his father was no fool. 'I just came around to tell you that I've been wrong about you, that's all.'

'Compared to who?' Max asked shrewdly.

'Richard Morrison.'

'Oh.' Max's face was expressionless.

'I tried everything I could, Dad. I tried to get rid of him. Honest.'

'Look, son.' Max' attitude softened. 'You'll just have

to face the fact that your mother and I might never get back together again.' He placed a hand on Danny's shoulder. 'Your mother and I have got different lives now. I mean, she's got every right to go out with other men, if that's what she wants – just as *I've* got every right to go out with other women.'

Danny was disappointed to hear his father speak this way; he had expected something . . . well, more positive. 'I knew you wouldn't understand,' he muttered.

'I do, son,' Max said gently. 'I do.'

'If you did, you'd come back.'

'Come on, Danny, be honest with me.' His grip tightened on Danny's shoulder. 'The only reason you want me back is to get rid of this Morrison character.'

No, his father was no fool. He had hit the nail right on the head, but Danny was not about to admit it.

His mother and Richard Morrison were seeing more and more of each other—and Danny felt increasingly helpless to do anything about it. They went out to dinner, to shows. He brought her *flowers*, for Pete's sake. He tried to be friendly with Danny, to make himself out as some sort of *pal*—but Danny wasn't having any of it. Danny resisted him all the way. His guard was up. No attack, however insidious, was going to get past *him*. And all the time, he himself was looking for an opening. He thought that one might present itself at the dinner party to which his mother had invited Jim Robinson and Helen Daniels next door so they could meet her precious Richard.

'I don't know why you're going to all this trouble?' She was making all sorts of fancy preparations, she had already suggested to Danny that he might spend the evening with Scott next door.

'Because they're my best friends, and I want them to meet Richard under happy circumstances.'

Which meant without him. 'It should be a great success then,' Danny remarked drily.

'Oh yes, it will,' Marie said with a certainty that took him slightly aback.

She had asked him to pop next door to the Robinsons to tell Helen Daniels to arrive a little later than had first been arranged. He was to explain that she was a little behind in her preparations. Helen smiled when he passed on the message, and said she perfectly understood, there was nothing worse than having guests turn up on the doorstep when one was still covered in flour or whatever and looking an absolute fright.

Jim Robinson was on the telephone. Danny could hear him in the background. 'Ah . . . that's very civil of you, Max, but not tonight. I've got a lot of work that needs sorting out . . . you know how it is.' He sounded most uncomfortable. Then, when he had hung up, and saw Danny in the kitchen, he looked it. 'Oh . . . Danny.' Danny knew there had been some sort of disagreement between Jim Ramsay and his father. He didn't know what it was all about – but with Max there was always something to be at loggerheads about. 'I didn't know you were here.'

'Was that my Dad then?' Danny asked him.

'Yes, it was. He suggested we get together and have a few beers. But . . .' he glanced at his mother-in-law . . . 'we've made other arrangements.'

Maria's dinner. Getting to know Mr Wonderful. Jim Robinson had lied to Max, had told him he had work to do. And everybody was criticising Danny for the way *he* behaved. Jim Robinson was looking guilty—and so he should, Danny thought. He had an idea. He decided to pay his father a visit.

Max was in, as Danny knew he would be, because, apart from work, there was precious little he did with himself these days since he had left home except drink beer, watch television and manage to make his flat look even more disorderly.

'I was just going over to see Jim Robinson,' Max told

Danny just after he arrived at the flat. 'Bury the hatchet, a few drinks. But he's busy. I don't want to interrupt him. You know what an old woman he can be about his work.'

Danny didn't know about burying the hatchet. He was more interested in burying something else, laying to rest once and for all a relationship that was threatening to get out of hand. 'Is that what he told you?'

'Yeah. Why?'

'Nothing,' Danny said quickly. 'Look, Dad,' he went on, 'if you're at a loose end why don't you go around and see Mum.'

Max looked doubtful. 'She's probably out with Richard Morrison,' he said. 'Besides, who says I'm at a loose end? There's plenty for me to do here.'

'She's home tonight,' Danny told him eagerly. 'She wouldn't mind you dropping in.'

'No, I don't think . . .'

Danny couldn't let it go at that. 'There's something I've been meaning to ask you. About my bike. The seat's jammed.'

'If you're angling for a new bike, you can forget it.' Max was obviously smelling the wrong rat. 'I just don't have the money'.

'It's not that, Dad,' Danny hurriedly assured him. 'I'm perfectly happy with this bike—honest. It's just that . . . well . . . the seat's pretty uncomfortable. And the brakes need checking.'

Max sighed. He had the air of a man who was being sorely put upon. 'All right then. I'll pop over tomorrow. How's that?'

No good at all. It had to be tonight. Danny thought quickly. 'I've got a school excursion tomorrow. I can't go if the bike's not roadworthy.'

'All right,' Max said after a thoughtful pause. 'But I've got to have my dinner first.'

'Fine' Danny said happily. 'You do that.'

Danny wanted to see what happened when his father turned up at Marie's dinner out of the blue and set the cat loose among the chickens. He wanted to be a silent witness to what transpired—but he could hardly do that at home. He had another idea—they were coming thick and fast tonight. From a public telephone box, he called Des Clarke who lived next door to the Ramsay house, on the other side from the Robinsons'. Could he come round? Sure, Des said, he wasn't doing anything, anyway. So Danny paid him a visit. From Des's place he should have a good view of what was happening next door.

Des was alone, watching television. Daphne was out somewhere. He asked Danny if he wanted to hang around anywhere, why didn't he do it in his own place. Danny replied that it was because his mother was having people for dinner, namely her boyfriend and Jim Robinson and Helen Daniels from next door. As he spoke, he kept parting Des's living room curtains a fraction and peering out to see if there was any sign yet of his father making an appearance.

'Are you practising for a play, or something?'

Danny let the curtain fall. 'How would you feel if your Dad's best friend told him a lie—just because of that Morrison guy?'

'You're talking about Jim Robinson—right?' Des eyed him levelly from the depths of his armchair. 'Maybe he's trying to *avoid* hurting your Dad,' he suggested. 'You know Jim and Max haven't been getting along too well lately. Now . . . why your big hate? I mean, you're only making your mother miserable.'

'I'm trying to make her see some sense,' Danny said, 'and get rid of him.'

'He can't be that bad,' Des observed.

'You haven't met him.'

'I know that.' Des was still regarding him evenly from his chair in front of the television on which the volume had been turned down. 'I know your mother, though. She's not the sort to get herself involved with some creep. So, okay—you get rid of him. Then what happens?'

'Maybe Dad and Shane would come home.'

'Don't be a fool, Danny. Your parents didn't split up because of Morrison. Their problems started a long time before that. You've got to accept that the marriage is over and stop making life miserable for yourself and your Mum.'

But Danny didn't want to believe that. He had already convinced himself that it was simply a matter of removing Morrison from the scene, and then everything would be back to normal. He lifted the curtain again. Surely, his father ... and yes, there he was, turning in through the gate of his house. Good, good, Danny thought exultantly; here went the neighbourhood. He only wished he could be there to witness the explosion once Max realised what was going on in his own house.

The dinner party was over. Danny liked to think it had broken up in a shambles, drink spilt if not your actual blood. From the front window of Des Clarke's house, Danny watched them leave—Max first, walking quickly away, obviously upset; then Jim Robinson and Helen Daniels. And Richard Morrison. . ? It didn't seem that he was ever going to leave. His car still stood, blackly ominous, outside the house. *He* was the one, Danny thought, who should have been the first to leave—beaten, cowed, lacerated by Max's razor-sharp tongue.

'Maybe he has decided to stay,' Des remarked.

'He must have rocks in his head if he's still hanging around,' Danny said, still watching the street outside. They were probably having a serious talk in there, Richard Morrison and his mother. Yes, that was it, Danny decided; he was telling her he was sorry . . . but things being as they were . . . she would understand . . . it just wouldn't work out, there were too many other factors . . .

Richard Morrison must have remained in the house for something like an hour after the others had gone. But, finally, he did leave, walking down the front path, briefly illuminated in the wedge of light from the hallway before the front door closed behind him. A few moments later, he was driving away, the red tail-lights diminishing before disappearing as he turned the corner at the end of the street. Danny gave it another fifteen minutes or so before deciding it was safe enough to return home. He didn't want to make it look too obvious.

His mother was on her hands in the living room, spraying something on the carpet then rubbing it vigorously with a cloth. So maybe blood had been spilt after all. Marie straightened, and glared at Danny. 'You know something about this, don't you?' she challenged him.

'About what?' Danny was acting the complete innocent; he knew nothing. 'What happened?' He gestured to the spot on the floor which she had been so vigorously scrubbing. 'Was there a fight?'

Maria was on her feet. She shook her head. 'No, no fight,' she said acidly. 'I'm sorry to disappoint you. This is liqueur, not blood.' Danny could tell she was furious. 'Why did you do it?' she cried.

'Mum, I . . .'

'You've never given Richard a chance, have you? And using Max like that . . . He was trying to be such a good father to you . . . and now look what you've done.' The dishes were still on the table. There was wine, and a vase of flowers that had no doubt been brought by *him*. The party must have been proceeding very nicely until the moment Max had come barging in to disrupt it. 'But your plan didn't work, Danny, I'm sorry to say.

You haven't affected Richard and me in the slightest. What you *have* done, though, is ruin the relationship between Jim and Max—and if I were Max, I would never forgive you.'

Max would have told her that Danny had led him to believe she was alone in the house. 'I only did it for you,' Danny said resentfully. 'Not that you'd care.'

'But I don't . . .' Maria was more exasperated now than angry. 'What made you do such a stupid thing?'

'Does it matter?' He was bitter. He was only trying to get his family back together again—no one seemed to appreciate that. 'You never listen, anyway.'

'I'm listening now.'

'I don't like the way we're living,' he said sullenly.

'You don't like Richard, you mean.' Maria moved closer to him. 'And what's wrong with having my own life?' she demanded. 'Why *can't* I be happy—just this once? It must always be you . . .' her finger jabbed towards him . . . '*you*. That's what you expect, isn't it?' she went on relentlessly. 'I'm supposed to give everything . . . my own happiness . . . just for you.'

'And so you should,' Danny blurted out. 'You're my *mother*. That's what you're *supposed* to do.'

It seemed that everyone was ganging up on him. Jim Robinson was the next one to have a go. Danny was just on his way to see if Scott Robinson was ready to accompany him to school when Jim began to back his car down the drive. Seeing Danny, he stopped the car and climbed out. Danny asked him if Scott was ready. Just about, Jim told him, then proceeded to give him a lecture.

'That was a pretty crazy stunt you pulled last night,' he said, and Danny knew that his mother—or perhaps it was Max, but that was hardly likely—had had a quiet word with him—and Jim, as always, had probably told her he would see what he could do to make Danny see reason. It would be just like him. 'Inviting your father to the house just made things difficult for everyone. Look . . .' Danny felt uncomfortable beneath the steadiness of Jim's gaze . . . 'if you *are* having trouble coming to terms with the situation, the best thing you can do is try and talk it over with someone.'

Oh yes, Danny thought wrily—and guess who was offering himself in the role of father confessor? 'Gee, thanks, Mister Robinson.'

Jim was clearly annoyed by the unmistakable sarcasm. 'You've caused me a great deal of trouble, Danny,' he said testily. 'Your father and I are not on the best of terms, and you're not helping. But apart from that, the only person you're hurting is your mother. She has her own life to lead, regardless of you and your manipulations. So why don't you shape up and start acting your age before you cause real trouble?'

Which was choice, coming from him. Two grown men at loggerheads about something or other—that was hardly what Danny called acting one's age.

He knew he would have to make it up with his father. That was essential. Max had to take a definite stand in all this—no matter what was going on between him and Jim Robinson which was really only a side issue after all.

'Set it all up, didn't you?' Max growled when Danny, full of trepidation, went to his flat. Shamefacedly, Danny had to admit he had—and waited for the abuse to start raining down on him. But instead of abuse, Max gave way to querulousness. 'But why? I mean, did you really *want* me to make such a fool of myself, barging in on their dinner party like that, yelling blue murder? Do you *really* hate me so much?'

'No, Dad.' Danny was feeling utterly miserable. 'That's not how it was at all.'

'How was it then?'

'I wanted you to take charge . . .' He had to make his father understand; to himself it was perfectly clear. 'I mean, with Mum. I want to see us all back together again.' It was a heartfelt plea. 'Can't you come home, Dad?'

Max turned away. 'I would if I could,' he said quietly. 'But I can't. I mean, your Mum's has someone else, doesn't she?'

'He's on the way out,' Danny promised. 'Honest.'

'Even so . . .' Max shook his head. He seemed to be affected by his son's entreaty. 'No, we never *could* get back together again.'

Dismayed by what he regarded as his father's defeatism, Danny stared at him. Max seemed uncomfortable. 'You haven't given up, have you?' Danny asked weakly. If his father had given up, then that made the battle all that much harder for Danny to wage. It made the odds impossibly high.

'No . . . no, of course not.' But Max didn't sound convincing.

It wasn't only Max's negativism, he was soon to discover, that was working against him. There were other factors in motion of which he didn't become aware until it was too late.

It was Scott who told him that Richard Morrison was going to Hong Kong. He had picked it up from his old man who, in his turn, had apparently been informed by Maria Ramsay. Danny was the last to hear about it, but that didn't matter. He was getting what he wanted after all. He couldn't believe his luck.

'Yes, that's right,' Maria told him. 'It's all been rather sudden. His company's representative there had a heart attack. Richard is being sent to replace him.' Now that it was confirmed, Danny resisted the urge to leap into the air, to do handsprings and somersaults, to yell with joy. It had all worked out very nicely. Who would have thought Hong Kong was crooking a seductive finger at the home-breaker? 'Danny . . . I want to go with him,' Maria said unhappily. 'And we want you to come with us.'

It was as if she had just given him a good solid kick in the groin. Worse than that. 'You *can't* go,' he whispered.

'I am Danny.' She looked pale but determined.

'You don't even know him?' Danny was floundering about, trying to find any argument—any argument at all.

'I do, Danny,' she said gravely. 'And I love him.'

Love him? What sort of nonsense was that? 'Can't you wait?'

'Wait for what?'

'Well . . . at least until he comes back from Hong Kong.'

'He's not coming back.'

This was getting worse. It was as if Danny had suddenly stepped into quicksand—and a moment ago he had been so chock-a-block full of excitement to think that Richard Morrison was fading right out of the picture. 'Well, *I'm* not going,' he said defiantly. 'I don't want to be with him.'

'You'll be with both of us,' Maria pointed out. 'Danny listen,. whatever you think about Richard—and he does like you, he'd like to get to know you better . . . and we've talked it over. We want you to come with us. We'll be a family.'

'Some family,' Danny snorted bitterly. 'You, me and him—and six million Chinese. And what about Shane?'

'Shane's old enough to look after himself.'

'So am I.'

'No, you're not.'

'Mum, I'm not a kid any more. I can take care of myself.'

'Please don't make a hasty decision,' Maria said unhappily. 'All I'm asking you is to take some time to consider Richard's offer.'

'And how long did *you* take?' Danny retorted. 'Five seconds?' He gestured brusquely. 'Forget it.'

'I can't forget it, Danny.' She was close to tears. 'I have to consider you.'

Danny was adamant. There was no way she could talk him into doing something he didn't want to do—which was to go to Hong Kong with Mr Richard Bloody Morrison. 'I can look after myself. And you . . . you can do what you want.' He had lost his mother—he knew that now for a fact; there was nothing he could do now to make her change her mind. But he still had his father, and Shane—they would move back to the house, and there would be the three of them, coping, having fights—oh, there would be plenty of fights with his father around— muddling along as best they could. It wouldn't be too bad. They would manage, somehow. 'You just do whatever you want,' he cried as he rushed headlong out of the kitchen.

Eight

Strange, inexplicable things were happening—and Daphne Lawrence soon came to believe the house was haunted. When the glass flew through the room, seemingly of its own volition, and shattered against the mantelpiece, she was sure of it.

It was just a little niggle at first, which began when she came back that night to find that the light was on when she was sure—quite certain, really—that she had turned it off before she left. Inside, she heard music which she tracked down to a transistor radio on the kitchen table. Leaving a radio on—that was something she would never do. Someone must have been there, turning on the light, switching on the radio . . . and what else? She experienced a start of panic. She checked the windows and doors, but they were all securely locked as she had left them. As far as she could tell, no one had broken into the house. Nothing had been taken. She told herself, although not altogether convincingly, that she was being foolish. Somebody breaking into the house just to listen to the radio? That was silly. She must have just forgotten to switch it off. But even so, it was quite out of character for her. Strange, she thought with a puzzled shake of her head.

She was really only just looking after the house for a few months while the owner was overseas. It had been something of a windfall for her. It was large enough, comfortable enough, convenient, and the rent was minimal. The real estate people had put her onto it. She had been looking for a place to live now that Des Clarke was talking seriously about getting married, which meant that there would no longer be room for her in the house she had been sharing with him on a strictly above board basis, and which now—or, after his marriage, the date for which had not yet been set—would have to be relinquished to the new Mrs Clarke and the twins from a previous marriage she was bringing with her as a dowry. Poor Des, Daphne had thought with a twinge of pleasure; the instant family man. Now she had her own house to look after—and strange things were happening.

If she could dismiss—although not entirely—the light and the radio that had been left on, she couldn't ignore the open window she discovered in the living room the following morning. She knew for a fact that she had locked it the night before; she had made sure of it before going upstairs to bed. Then, on top of that, there was the empty orange juice carton in the refrigerator. She had bought it only the day before, and it hadn't been opened. It was a worry; there was definitely something strange going on.

Then, abruptly, her puzzlement changed to alarm when, in quick succession, two slices of toast popped up in the toaster, something was knocked over in the next room, and then the chandeliers began to move as the bumps came from upstairs. It was as if someone were jumping up and down on the floor of the room above. By that time Daphne had rushed into the room where something had been knocked over, and saw the tall floor lamp lying on its side. She was suddenly very frightened. She telephoned Shane Ramsay who said he would be right over. In the meantime, he suggested she call the police.

Terrified of staying alone in the house where these strange things were happening, she waited in the back garden for the police to arrive. Of course, she hadn't been imagining it, she told herself over and over again; there had definitely been bumps, the lamp was still lying

116

on its side, toast had popped up in the toaster, and somebody had drunk her orange juice.

'Hello there.' The voice came from behind her. Her nerves stretched to their limit as they were, she started. A young man with unkempt hair was grinning at her over the fence.

'Oh . . . hello.'

'I thought Mister Burns was away.'

'He is,' Daphne told him. 'I'm house-sitting.' She gestured towards the house in question. 'I think there's someone in there.'

'Really?' Suddenly the young man was looking serious.

Daphne nodded. 'I'm waiting for the police.'

'Should I go and have a look?'

'Better not. He could be dangerous.' Whoever it was in there, on the rampage.

'You can come and stay in here if you like.' The young man jerked his head towards the house behind him.

'No, it's all right. Thanks. I'd better stay here. The police will be here soon.'

When the police arrived, two of them with rather grim expressions, they found nothing. They looked upstairs and downstairs. They opened cupboards and peered inside wardrobes. They were very thorough.

'Have they found anything yet?' Shane Ramsay asked when he arrived a few minutes later.

'No,' one of the policemen told him. 'All we've really got is an open window. It's hardly the crime of the century.'

About half an hour later, without having turned up anything, the policemen left after advising Daphne to give the station a call if she happened to notice anyone suspicious in the area—or anything suspicious, for that matter.

'I know they don't believe me,' Daphne said woefully after they had gone.

'They didn't have much to go on, did they?' Shane pointed out.

'He must have hidden somewhere while I was waiting outside.'

'Come on, Daphne.' Shane was looking at her doubtfully.

'You don't believe me, either, do you?'

'But where could they be?' If Shane was trying to help, he wasn't making much of a fist of it. Daphne knew what she knew. She *knew* there had been someone playing merry havoc inside the house. She looked back at him reproachfully. 'I mean, you didn't see a car drive off, or anyone run out the back.'

That was true. 'But there's plenty of room to hide in the garden.' It was a spacious garden, with plenty of trees and bush to offer concealment for anyone. 'Look, Shane, I wouldn't make up a story like this. Why should I?'

Shane thought about this for a moment. 'All right then. Fair enough. So what do you do now?'

That was something that had been bothering her. What *did* she do now? She certainly didn't want to be alone in the house—not before this whole thing had been resolved in one way or another. And if the place *was* haunted, which was another strong possibility that presented itself, then . . . 'Unless we catch whoever it is red-handed. Perhaps . . .' she looked at him intently. 'If you were to stay with me tonight . . . You could use one of the spare bedrooms.' She touched his hand. 'Please, Shane. I just can't stand the thought of being alone.'

'All right,' Shane said after a brief pause. 'I'll come over after work.'

But when Shane turned up that evening, carrying an overnight bag, he told her he would be back later as he had to pick up someone from the airport. In the meantime, he had just popped in to see if she was all right. Daphne wasn't very happy about the thought of spending even a couple of hours alone in the house at night—but she knew she had no choice.

After he had gone, she tried to read, but she couldn't concentrate. She was hearing all sorts of sounds, creaks and whispers which her greatly overworked imagination magnified into monstrous, sinister and stealthy goings-on all around her, no matter how hard she tried to convince herself that they were just the normal sounds of the early evening, trees rustling in the breeze outside, distant traffic, the vague contractions of a very old house. But, as she thought later when she had calmed down sufficiently to put the incident into some perspective, no wild stretch of the imagination could account for the glass tumbler that suddenly came sailing through the room to shatter against the mantelpiece. She screamed.

The police arrived, and once again they found nothing after thoroughly searching the house from top to bottom. And as before, Daphne could tell by their sceptical expressions that they didn't believe her. After they had gone, and she was sweeping up the broken glass while wishing Shane would hurry because there was no knowing what would happen next in this mysterious house, there was a knock at the front door. Her heart began to palpitate again.

'Who is it?' she called timorously from the hallway.

'It's me. Next door. Colin.'

Relieved, Daphne opened the door to the young man with the unkempt hair who had spoken to her over the back fence earlier that day.

'I just saw the police leave,' he explained. 'I gather you've had another . . . incident.'

If that was what he wanted to call it. 'I wish I knew what was happening here,' Daphne said.

'You can come over to our place if you like,' Colin suggested. 'Mum and Dad wouldn't mind.'

'My friend, Shane, will be over shortly,' she told him. 'I think I'll survive until then.' She was most grateful for the offer.

'Then I'll stay until he comes. You don't mind, do you?'

'I'll be very grateful.'

'I think I'll rather enjoy being a knight in shining armour,' he said cheerfully. 'That is, until the real one comes along.'

Daphne liked him. He was very friendly, and thoughtful. She thought he could be quite fun.

When Shane turned up about an hour later, Daphne was feeling perfectly relaxed in Colin's company. He had told her jokes and made her laugh. She had been right—he *was* fun. Shane looked displeased. 'How well do you know that bloke?' he demanded after Colin had gone. Daphne had a shrewd guess that he had expected her to throw herself into his manly and protective arms—but instead of that, here she was in the company of some guy, enjoying herself, looking quite relaxed.

'Well enough,' she replied. 'He was cheering me up.'

'I don't know,' Danny said tersely. 'Here you are, worried that there's some lunatic loose in the house— and you let a stranger walk in. You hardly know anything about him.'

That was true—but she was quite sure about Colin. She was also sure that Shane was experiencing pangs of jealousy.

She fixed dinner for them both. Afterwards they nestled cosily on the couch. 'This place is getting to be a bit of a hassle for you, isn't it?' Shane observed.

'It is, a little.' She had been so excited when she moved in. A place of her own, to come and go as she pleased. But now . . . Bumps in the night, shattering glass.

'Then find somewhere else.'

'And run away? I don't think so.'

120

He had his arm around her. 'You know, I can't come running every time you hear a noise,' he said. 'I might be doing something else.'

Disengaging herself from his encircling arm, Daphne leapt to her feet. 'Well, thank you very much,' she exclaimed. 'I didn't realise it was such a chore. So please don't put yourself out on my account.' He really did annoy her at times. He had the knack of saying the wrong thing.

Shane was also on his feet. 'Please, Daphne. Don't be silly.' He followed her into the living room. 'Let's face it, you didn't seem to need my company when I arrived.'

'I thought you *wanted* to come over.'

'I did, but . . .'

She rounded on him. 'Then you can just go again,' she cried angrily. 'I can look after myself.'

'I damn well feel like it.' His own voice was raised.

'Then what's stopping you?'

'You are.' He moved across to the couch. 'I said I would stay the night—and I'm staying. I'm not having you accuse me of running out when you needed help.' He sat down on the couch.

'Well, I don't want you here,' Daphne snapped.

'Too bad.' Shane stretched himself full length on the couch. 'Goodnight.'

Daphne stared at him for a moment, then, her expression softening, she shook her head. There were times, too, when he could be totally irresistible.

Daphne slept well that night. In the morning, she made tea and toast for Shane who complained he had slept hardly at all. 'You should have slept in one of the beds,' she said, setting the tray down beside him.

'Yeah . . . well.' Shane sipped his tea, ate his toast. Daphne had already decided to fix herself something later. There was a knock at the front door. 'No guesses who *that* is,' Shane said with a groan.

Daphne opened the door to Colin from next door. He was very bright and breezy this morning. 'Hi, gorgeous,' he greeted her. 'I've come to invite you for breakfast. Bacon and eggs, toast. A hearty breakfast was had by all. What do you say?'

'Sounds fine.'

Shane was standing near the living room door, eyeing the newcomer with disapproval. 'I've got to rush off,' he said to Daphne.

'Okay. Call me later.'

She had breakfast with Colin in the house next door. She met his mother who fussed over her, and his father who read his newspaper. Feeling much better after she had eaten, she was returning to her own house through the back gate when she suddenly heard a faint sound coming from close by. She stopped and listened. She heard it again. It was definitely coming from the house. A slither? A bump? A scratching sound? She couldn't identify it. It was very close. Her heart skidded, the breath caught in her throat. She pressed her back against the wall. No, she wasn't imagining it.

There was a rake leaning against the wall. She grabbed it and moved silently along the wall. The steps leading down to the cellar door were just in front of her. Was the sound coming from down there? She couldn't be sure. Brandishing the rake, she moved stealthily down the steps to the cellar door. She was holding her breath. She was very frightened. She pushed against the door. It didn't budge. She pushed harder.

The cellar door was immovable. She leaned against it, and listened, but she could no longer hear the sound. So perhaps it *had* been her imagination after all. It was a thought that brought with it some relief. She walked back up the steps.

She had just reached the top of the steps when she froze. This time the sound was more definite, identifiable—the sound of breaking glass, and it had come from ... Fearfully, Daphne looked towards where she was sure it had come from.

There was another small door set into the wall of the house near the back steps. She had not noticed it before; it was partially concealed by bushes. But from this angle ... With her back against the wall, she crept towards this door which probably opened into a storage space for firewood or coal or whatever. Reaching the door, she pressed herself flat against the wall, one hand holding the rake as an improvised weapon, the other reaching out for the door catch. It was now or never ... It took her a moment to prepare herself. Her hand was hovering over the catch. Now ... Grasping hold of the catch, she pushed it upwards. Released, the door swung inwards a fraction. Daphne pushed it further with her foot.

It happened so quickly, a sudden rush of movement, something darting past her into the open, that Daphne was completely caught off guard. But she was quick to rally. With a yelp of alarm, she reacted instinctively and, dropping the rake, set off after the slight figure that had so abruptly emerged from its hidey-hole beneath the house. In front of her, the figure slipped on the path and lost its balance. Catching up, Daphne grabbed hold of it and pushed it up against the wall. Only then did she realise that it was a young girl of about fourteen or fifteen.

'Who the devil are you?' Daphne demanded, her fear now replaced by a rising anger. To think that this ... this *kid* had been responsible for frightening the wits out of her. 'What are you doing here?'

The girl stared back at her with profound insolence. She wasn't struggling, or screaming; she just glared at Daphne who was still holding her in a tight grip. The girl was thin-faced, her hair was straggly and her large eyes expressive of her scorn. 'I've been here for ages.'

So it *was* her. Daphne suppressed the urge to laugh

outright, so great was her relief that she was dealing with flesh and blood and not some mischief-making phantom. Or an escaped convict bent on mayhem. 'I *thought* someone was playing games.'

'I bet you thought the house was haunted.' As Daphne relaxed her grip, the girl tried to break away—but Daphne caught her again.

'I did not.' It wasn't true, but she wasn't prepared to admit that. 'I thought it was a prowler.' She studied the creature she had pinned against the wall. 'You still haven't told me who you are.'

'You were pretty scared, weren't you?' the girl said with a sneer. 'I saw you. You didn't know *what* was happening.'

'You're a bit too smart for your own good, young lady,' Daphne said coldly. 'Now, either you start giving me some answers, or I call the police.'

'You've called them before, and they didn't believe you.'

Daphne eyed her narrowly. 'So you were here all the time, were you?'

'Sure I was.' The girl's smile was irritatingly smug. 'Upstairs. I heard every word.'

Daphne released the girl. She didn't think she would make another attempt to escape. 'Why? Why pick on me? I've never done anything to you. I don't even know you.'

The girl seemed to be weighing her up, perhaps wondering if she should trust Daphne or not. Finally, she said, 'My name's Rachel. I was living here before you moved in.'

That could mean anything. 'Squatting?' Daphne asked.

'I suppose . . .' The girl, Rachel, pursed her lips as she considered just what it was she had been doing in the house. 'No, not exactly.'

'Then what?' Daphne was beginning to lose

patience. The girl was being deliberately obtuse.

'I don't *have* to tell you anything,' Rachel muttered defiantly.

Daphne clutched the upper part of the girl's arm. 'You listen to me,' she grated through clenched teeth. 'You've been breaking and entering. You could have been stealing.'

'I was not,' Rachel protested.

'Then why did you go to all the trouble to frighten me the way you did?'

'Because I wanted to get you out of here,' Rachel answered simply.

'But I'm renting the place.' Daphne was even more puzzled. 'I've got a perfect right to be here.'

'So have I. This is my home.'

'What do you mean? *Your* home?' Rachel said nothing. 'All right then,' Daphne said. 'Why don't we go inside and have a cup of tea?'

Rachel looked startled by the suggestion. 'You're not going to throw me out, are you?' she asked suspiciously.

'Not immediately.' Daphne told her. 'But I'm thinking about it.'

It took some time to get the story. Daphne was patient. As they drank their tea, she quietly questioned the girl, who eventually came forth with the information that her name was Rachel Burns.'

'Burns?' The name sounded familiar.

'Yes. Don't you remember who you rented the house from?'

'Of course.' It came back now. 'It didn't register for a moment.'

'My father.'

'But he's gone overseas.'

'I know,' Rachel said solemnly. 'I'm living with my mother—and my stepfather.' She made a grimace of distaste. 'I can't stand him.'

'Who?'

'My stepfather.'

'But what does that have to do with your being here?'

Rachel had her cup cradled in both hands. 'I had to get away from him. My stepfather. I knew my real Dad was overseas and that this place was empty. What I *didn't* know was that it had been rented out to you.'

'I see.'

The girl was staring at her wide-eyed over the rim of her cup. 'You do believe me, don't you?'

Daphne nodded. 'I believe you. But that still doesn't excuse what you did.'

Putting down her cup, Rachel stood up and began to pace the room. 'I had to do *something*,' she cried. 'You don't know what it's like, being forced to live with someone you don't like. I want to be with my Dad.' She was trembling, close to tears. 'He should be here. They should have let me go with him.' She swung to face Daphne. 'This is my home.'

Daphne could see that the girl was struggling to keep herself under control. 'Hasn't your mother tried to find you?' she asked. 'I mean, if I were her, this would be the first place I'd look.'

'She did.' Rachel's smile was brief but complacent. 'She rang one day when you were out. I answered the phone. She didn't know it was me. I changed my voice. I pretended to be you.'

The little horror. Daphne glared at her. 'Who do you think you are?' she demanded.

The girl's cockiness was back again. 'Like I said, this is more my house than yours.' She held Daphne's stare for a moment. 'Why are you looking at me like that?'

'I'm not sure,' Daphne replied flatly. 'For a moment there, I was beginning to feel sorry for you.'

'Well, you can stuff that.'

'Don't you dare speak to me like that.' Daphne was on her feet. She was livid. She grabbed the girl's arm.

'Sorry.' From her tone, she was anything but that.

'Rubbish,' Daphne said harshly. 'How many times have you intercepted my phone calls?'

'Only the once. That was from my mother.'

'How can I get in touch with your mother?'

'You're not serious, are you?'

'Of course I'm serious. She must be out of her mind with worry.'

Rachel shrugged. 'If she *really* cared, she would have found me by now.'

'And anyway,' Daphne said firmly, 'you're under age. I'm not accepting responsibility for you under this roof unless she knows where you are.'

'Well, you don't expect me to tell you where she is, do you?'

'I could call the police.'

'You won't do that,' Rachel said with certainty.

'Or the real estate people.'

'I'm sure they'd like to know that you had a man stay here last night.'

Daphne was furious. The little . . . 'I ought to belt the living daylights out of you.'

'You wouldn't want to try,' Rachel said smugly.

Daphne slumped back onto her chair. It seemed, like it or not, she was stuck with this Rachel Burns for the time being, probably until her father arrived back from overseas, whenever that would be. 'How old are you, anyway?' she asked. 'Fourteen?'

'Fifteen. Most people say I look older.'

Daphne didn't know about that. She was still just a kid to her. 'You don't *act* older.'

Rachel sat down at the table opposite her. 'Who cares?'

'And if I *do* let you stay . . .'

'You don't have much choice.'

'Oh, yes I do,' Daphne snapped. 'Let's get that straight from the start. I'll let you stay until you've had time to sort things out in your own mind. And while you're here, you'll keep me informed where you are, who you're with and what you're doing at all times.'

Rachel stared at her in amazement. 'You're kidding.'

'And you're fifteen,' Daphne retorted.

'You're treating me like a kid,' Rachel said sullenly.

'You *are* a kid. And while you're here, you're my responsibility.'

'You sound like my mother.'

'Then she must have really cared about you.'

Rachel quickly changed the subject. 'Is that it? Or do you have some more rules and regulations to dump on me?'

'No. That's about it.' Daphne's voice softened. 'I want to know where I can contact your mother.'

'No way.' Rachel shook her head decisively.

'Suppose you have an accident? Or fall sick?' When Rachel remained silent, she said, 'I'll only call her if I have to.'

Rachel thought about this. 'Okay,' she said at last.

'Good.' Daphne smiled across the table at her. 'Now that we understand each other we might just get along.'

'Do you think so?' Suspicion still lurked in the girl's eyes.

'Why not?' Daphne was beginning to feel quite cheerful. 'Female company could be nice for a change.'

Nine

Max didn't believe it. It couldn't be. Not Amy Medway, not her of the school swimming team—and who ever minded when she won? But there it was, her name on the back of the envelope, written in an elegant flowing hand. Amy Medway who could dive like a dolphin with scarcely a splash as her body cleaved the water, the belle of the school ball, writing to *him*. At school she had been a looker, a stunner, a real knockout—and now, in her maturity? He was suffused by a delicious tingle. He sniffed the letter. Softly perfumed . . . ah, spring blossom. He tore open the envelope. Amy Medway, the girl who quickened the adolescent heart was back in town and wanted him to telephone her—which, nervously, feeling a little guilty about it, he did.

'Oh, Max, how nice to hear from you.' A gentle seductive lilt on the other end of the line from the woman who had sent him a perfumed letter through the mail.

'Yeah.' Max felt quite tongue-tied. 'Yeah.'

'And how have you been? It's been so many years.'

'I keep myself pretty fit.' He had a vision of limpid eyes, long silky blonde hair, and lips that promised the world—the same lips that were now moulding words for his ears alone.

'I still swim every day,' she told him.

'Good. I'm getting divorced.'

'You, too?'

'One of those things.'

129

'You heard about the school reunion?' she asked, this sultry creature on the other end of the line.

'Maybe we should have one of our own,' Max suggested. You're a bold one, he said to himself.

'What a marvellous idea.' A tinkle of laughter. A ripple of bells. 'When?'

'Ah . . .' Don't overdo it, Max, don't be too eager. 'I'll just check my diary.'

'What about tomorrow night?'

'Yeah, fine.' Twenty years at least since he had last seen her—and, no, a drink together would do no harm at all. An interesting experience to catch up with some old school chum, particularly one with skin as smooth and as golden as honey.

So he arranged to meet Amy Medway in the Yardarm Bar at seven the following night. Max wondered if he would recognise her. What if she *had* changed beyond recognition? Twenty years was a long time. She told him she would be wearing a red silk dress—and that sounded reasonable enough. No mistaking a red silk dress in the gloom of the Yardarm Bar at seven o'clock in the evening. They said goodbye, see you then, and Max waited for a moment in front of the coin-operated telephone in the hall outside his flat for it to spit his money back at him. He had certainly hit the jackpot tonight, he decided.

So it was that at a few minutes before seven the following night, dressed in his best suit, he was sitting on a stool in the Yardarm Bar, chatting amicably to Jack the barman whom he knew quite well. He was a little nervous. He kept glancing towards the entrance of the bar which was all plush and glittering brasswork since it had been done up for the purpose of attracting a better type of clientele. Apart from Max there was only one other customer in the bar, a man seated on a stool in the far corner who kept glancing at his watch as if he, too, was expecting someone.

'Do you know what I'd do if I was Ronald Reagan,' Jack the barman said as he placed a light beer in front of Max.

'What would you do?' So this was going to be one of those serious and philosophical discussions the like of which had taken place even before the Yardarm Bar was refurbished. 'Blow the place up?'

'No.' Jack the barman was leaning on his folded arms in front of him. 'I'd declare a national referendum on unilateral disarmament.'

Of course you would, Max thought, looking at him. 'Reckon that'd work?'

'Who knows?' Jack the barman regarded Max solemnly. 'If the Russians did the same, we'd all be laughing.'

'Peace at last, eh?' Max nodded slowly. 'Have you got any cashews?'

'You know,' Jack the barman went on, 'it never ceases to amaze me. I mean, the number of people I get in here going on about how we're all going to be wiped off the face of the earth by a nuclear war.'

Max looked around at the virtually deserted bar. It might already have happened. The fellow in the corner was morosely sipping his beer. 'It's a serious problem, Jack,' Max agreed. 'I've got kids I care about. I want to see them grow up.'

'Yeah, and do you know what I say to them? Wasn't World War Two enough for you? How many wars do you want?'

'You've got a point,' Max said. 'Good point.'

'And do you know how I reckon we could stop wars? If families stop fighting—that's what I reckon.'

This was getting a little close to home. Max glanced at the door to see if there was any sign yet of Amy Medway, swimming champion. 'Sounds a bit simple, Jack.'

'What if everyone said, I forgive you.'

Very philosophical indeed. 'They'd probably say you're some sort of nut. Speaking of which . . .'

'The cashews. Right. I heard you. I'd rather be a nut than non-existent.

Amy Medway was late. It was already after seven. Jack the barman chatted on. Since it had been transformed, the Yardarm Bar was obviously a lonely place. 'People are completely out of touch with who they are,' he observed. 'You can't blame the politicians. They're only as good as we are.'

'That's right.' Max chewed his cashew nuts which Jack the barman had emptied into a bowl for him. In the old days there had been no bowls for the cashew nuts, but the place had been full of people.

'Do you want another?'

'Yeah, why not?' Max pushed his empty glass across the counter. 'We've got to live a bit more simply, put a bit more quality into our lives instead of quantity.' He had a sneaking suspicion that the observation wasn't altogether original; he might have picked it up from somewhere.

Jack the barman placed a fresh glass of beer in front of him. 'You know the least thing we give ourselves?'

'What's that?'

'Love.'

'Yeah?' Could he fall in love with Amy Medway—*if* she came? She was already ten minutes late.

'And love is the first thing we all say we want the most. Crazy, isn't it?'

'Sure is,' Max drank some of his beer. 'We give ourselves a hard time.'

She was standing him up. Something else had come up, and she wasn't coming. He decided that if she hadn't come by the time he had finished his beer, he would leave and go home to ponder the fickle nature of women who swam like veritable mermaids. He glanced back at the door, and there, materialising out of the gloom into the gloom . . . oh no. 'I reckon the greatest ecological problem we've got today is soil erosion,' Jack the barman was saying, but Max wasn't listening to him. Max was aghast. Quickly, he picked up the newspaper he had brought into the bar with him and held it up so that she wouldn't see his face. She was wearing a red dress all right. It *had* to be her.

'And if you consider how the timber industry . . .' Max slid off his stool.

She was *huge* . . . oh God, she was huge. Huge and fierce looking. Where was the lissome grace, the style, the cool elegance he remembered? All gone, ploughed under beneath layers of fat, an archaeological nightmare. Stealthily, still holding up the late final edition of that evening's newspaper, Max made his way past this apparition to the door.

It had been a close shave. Disaster had been narrowly averted. He was in a very black mood by the time he reached his flat where the first thing he did was take Amy's letter from his pocket, regard it sourly for a moment then crumple it into a tight little ball. The telephone rang in the hall.

'It's Amy.' My, how a woman's voice could deceive. Who would think that the owner of such a voice . . .? Max closed his eyes to blot out the image.

'Oh, Amy. Hello.' He couldn't show any enthusiasm. A bitter blow had been dealt.

'Didn't you get my message? About being late?'

There had been no message. There had only been Jack the barman talking with relish about nuclear holocausts and the problem of soil erosion. 'No, I didn't.'

'I'm sorry. Did you wait long?'

Long enough. 'It doesn't matter,' Max muttered.

'Look, it's not late,' Amy said. 'We could still go out. Why don't I come to your place and pick you up?'

'No.' Max almost screamed the word. 'Ah . . . no, I don't think so. I'm a bit tired tonight, you see.' A good enough excuse; anybody could be tired; nothing unusual about that. 'You know how it is.'

'Then when can we get together?' She was being persistent, damn her, this mountainous woman in the red dress. Max thought quickly.

'Ah . . . you see . . . it would be difficult. I'm going to be tied up for the next few weeks. I'm going overseas. So . . . then . . . yes . . . I'll give you a call when I get back.' After that she couldn't help but realise that she was being given the brush-off. Her curt goodbye, then the very definite click in his ear confirmed this. 'Flaming women,' Max growled as he replaced the receiver.

A couple of days later, when he was having a drink with Jim Robinson in the Yardarm, the subject of Amy Medway was introduced into the conversation when Jim asked Max if he intended going to the forthcoming school reunion.

'I don't know,' Max replied. 'Half of me wants to, but the other half doesn't want to run into Amy Medway.'

'Why not?' Jim looked at him in surprise, then became reminiscent. 'Oh yes, Amy Medway. I remember her. Who could forget her? Pencil-thin. Artistry from the diving board. I haven't thought about her in years.'

'I wouldn't bother starting up again, if I were you,' Max said drily.

They were sitting side by side on stools at the counter. They were the only customers in the bar. 'Why Amy Medway all of a sudden?' Jim wanted to know.

'Ran into her last week,' Max said glumly.

'Really?' Jim's face lit up. 'How is she?'

'Hardly recognised her. Looks like the back end of a bus.'

The two men were silent for a moment. Behind the counter, Jack the barman was rearranging bottles on the shelves in front of the mirror that reflected the thoughtful images of Max and Jim. 'We're all getting older, mate,' Jim remarked at last.

Jack turned away from the shelves. 'Older, but not much wiser, eh, Max?' he said with a knowing smile.

'That's a bit uncalled for, Jack,' Max said a little gruffly.

'I don't know what's got into you lately.' Jack leaned on the counter in front of them.

'What do you mean?'

'That lady who came in here looking for you the other night. She said she'd arranged to meet you here. A real looker she was, very stylish.'

'Very funny, Jack,' Max growled.

'No, seriously.' Jack looked at Jim. 'She was. She came in here looking for him—and where was he? Probably at home with his feet in a couple of buckets of hot water.'

'You're having us on, Jack,' Max muttered.

'Not at all. A very nice looking lady she was. She asked if you had left any message for her. She said her name was Amy . . .' he tried to remember . . . 'Amy something. Amy Metcalf, something like that.'

'Amy Medway,' Jim supplied.

'That's right.' Jack the barman grinned at Max who was still quite convinced he was having his leg pulled. 'Amy Medway.'

But then, as Jack the barman continued to insist that he wasn't pulling his leg, Max began to think that he might be right after all—and if he *were* right, then a terrible mistake had been made. Perhaps he had been too anxious to escape the clutches of the wrong woman altogether. Mistaken identity. Another woman in a red dress. He remembered there had been another guy in the Yardarm Bar that night—a busy night for the Yardarm Bar—who had kept glancing at his watch as if he were expecting someone.

'You're always in the place you fear,' Jack the

barman told him cryptically. 'If you fear it, you're in it.'

'I'm not afraid, Jack,' Max said quietly. 'I'm cringing with embarrassment.'

Jim Robinson laughed. 'Oh, for heaven's sake, Max, Amy was always a pretty good sort of person. She'll understand. Give her a call and explain what happened. She'll probably think it's funny. I know I do.'

Both him and Jack the barman; they were having a quiet chortle. Max didn't think it was funny at all. It was bloody tragic, that's what it was. He had given the brush-off to the school diving champion. She had hung up in his ear. Big joke.

'It *is* funny when you come to think about it,' Jack the wise barman observed. 'How long have I known you two?'

'A good few years now, mate,' Jim Robinson replied. Since the good old days when the Yardarm Bar was bursting at the seams and the price of beer was nowhere near a dollar.

Leaning on the counter, Jack the barman looked from one of them to the other as he launched into his soliloquy. 'The trouble with you blokes is that you're both lonely. Outside of your families, what have you got?' He didn't wait for an answer to this, but bowled merrily on. 'The truth is, you could both do with a bit of female company.' He regarded Max with some sadness. 'Then this perfectly good-looking woman who obviously possesses bags of charm comes along—and what do you do? You do a bunk. You run as if your life depended on it. A right bolt, an unholy scarper. You make an undignified exit.' He shook his head in reproach. 'I don't know. Nobody ever listens to me.'

'Have you finished?' Max asked him.

'I think so.'

'Then I'd better make a phone call,' Max said, sliding off his stool and heading for the telephone in the corner.

'Amy?'

'Max.' There was no lilt in her voice today. It was flat, dull. 'I'm very busy, Max,' she said, and that was that. A click in his ear and a buzzing sound. Max put back the receiver. He had done his dash with that one.

'Well, that's the first step over and done with,' Jack the barman said brightly when he returned.

'I don't think I'll bother with the second,' Max said dispiritedly as he eased himself back up onto the stool.

'Give me the number,' Jim Robinson said. 'I'll ring her tomorrow.'

'She's all yours, mate,' Max said, handing him the slip of paper on which he had written Amy's number. 'All yours.'

Later, he was to tell himself that it was just a figure of speech he had used, something one said without really meaning it. He hadn't meant it literally. But that evening, about a week after he had made his magnanimous offer which wasn't an offer at all, if only people wouldn't take him seriously all the time, when he breasted into the Yardarm for a drink and Jack the barman told him his mate, namely Jim, was sitting over there in the corner—and Jack was looking fairly smug as he said it—and Max looked at the couple at the table, all wrapped up in each other, smiling and laughing and looking into each other's eyes, Max felt the twisting knife of betrayal. In the otherwise deserted bar, there was his so-called mate, and . . . and . . . she had changed hardly at all in the past twenty years. The same silky blonde hair caught the rippling light, the same eyes mirrored her noble soul, the same sensual lips whispered into Jim's shell-like ear. Yes, and the same honey-gold skin of the school swimming champion, provocative, exciting, a little fuller in the body perhaps, but all the better for that, who could probably still dive like a dolphin with scarcely a splash as she hit the water.

'There, you see?' Jack the barman said with infuriating smugness. 'I told you she was a looker.'

Max glared at the couple who, so intent on each other, were oblivious to his presence. 'The dirty double-crossing rat,' he said with feeling.

Ten

Douglas Blake was a man who seemed to have everything. He had grace and charm, and sterling good looks. He was witty and urbane, and very knowledgeable about art. Helen Daniels soon found herself quite captivated by him.

He had introduced himself at the bank which was staging an exhibition of Helen's paintings. He had admired her paintings, talked about landscapes and seascapes, perspectives and meanings. They had discussed traditionalists, impressionists and surrealists. He had given her his card which stated that he was an Art Advisor—meaning that he gave advice to art galleries, businesses, including banks, and individuals—and over coffee, offered to help her stage a proper exhibition which would bring her to the attention of a larger, art-loving public. Helen was excited by the prospect. Her painting had been more of a hobby, really; she had never given any thought to having exhibitions of it. It was only because Des Clarke had talked her into it that she had allowed the small selection of her paintings to be shown at the bank where he was Assistant Manager. Now here was this perfectly charming silver-haired man with the hawk-like profile telling her that her art deserved a wider public. It was something that had never occurred to her before.

'What will it cost?' Jim Robinson asked her that same evening.

Helen had been contemplating a selection of her paintings which she had propped up against the living room wall. She looked up at her son-in-law. 'What do you mean?'

'Well, it has to cost something. The gallery will have to be rented. There will be advertising, invitations to send out. Even if this Douglas fellow helps you, there'll be remounting, new frames.'

'I never thought of that,' Helen said with a frown. It could add up to quite an amount.

'I'm not saying it isn't possible,' Jim said.

Helen was sure it was possible. Artists were having exhibitions all the time. She was having dinner with Douglas the following night. She would ask him then.

'Not a thing,' Douglas told her when she asked him how much the exhibition would cost.

'Don't be silly.' They were sitting in a small, elegant restaurant with candles on the tables. Douglas had told her it was one of his favourite restaurants.

'You're the painter,' he said. 'I'm the exhibitor.'

'But the invitations, the reframing . . .'

'All my department,' he assured her.

'Are you sure?'

'Absolutely,' he said as the waiter came to take their order.

He had already told her he was a widower. He now encouraged her to talk about herself. He said he admired her for devoting her life to someone else's family. He thought it was a courageous thing for her to do. Helen didn't agree with that. Nor could she accept the notion that it was someone else's family.

'My daughter and Jim loved each other so much that I couldn't leave him to sink or swim after she died.'

'Of course not,' Douglas Blake said quickly over the Beef Wellington. 'But you must have had plans of your own. Painting. Travelling.'

Yes, there had been plans—once. 'I don't begrudge them a minute.'

'I'm sure you don't. You wouldn't be the type.'

She smiled faintly. 'Bill . . . that was my husband . . . we both loved the French Impressionists. We
had been planning for years to go to Paris where we
would stay for a couple of months before travelling
south and renting a small village at Arles.' Bitter-sweet
memories. They had been full of plans. 'Then, quite
suddenly, Bill died. I did think, some years later, of
going by myself, but then Anne, my daughter, Jim's
wife . . . she died sooner after Lucy was born. Jim was
shattered. So was I, but I suppose when it has already
happened once . . . a person becomes stronger, more
capable.'

'Yes.' Douglas nodded slowly. He would have his
own bitter-sweet memories, Helen thought. 'But now,
with the children growing up, you'll have to find new
interests.' He refilled her wine glass from the bottle of
Chardonnay he had ordered. 'You have to spread
yourself, expand.

Perhaps, she thought as she sipped her wine, she was
in something of a rut—but it was a very nice and
comfortable rut if that was what in fact it was.

When he came to the house the following morning to
see the pictures she had selected for the exhibition he
was so intent on arranging, Douglas told her he was
impressed. He looked closely at the eight landscapes in
oil she had picked out, nodded and seemed eminently
satisfied. 'Yes, I think they should do very nicely,' he
remarked. Then, smiling at her, he said, 'You know,
this has been a pure pleasure, and good for my ego. It's
not every day that one has the privilege of . . .
discovering a new talent, as it were.'

Helen laughed. 'You flatter me.'

'Flattery has nothing to do with it,' he said with mock
severity. 'I want very much to turn you into a successful
artist, and I believe that is a real possibility.'

'I'd be happy if I just sold one of them,' Helen said.

'A broad canvas, my dear,' he said with a chuckle.

'That's what you need. Heroic brushstrokes. You must be positive. You'll sell them all.' He waggled a finger in front of her nose. 'You mark my words. This could really be the start of something for you.'

Helen decided she liked him very much.

They were seeing quite a lot of each other. He took her out to lunch and to dinner. He told her he was still looking for a suitable gallery in which to hold the exhibition of her paintings. One day, he took her for a drive in the country. It was a fine, sunny day. 'I thought it might be nice to forget about art for the day, he told her. 'Or rather, the business side of art. We could spend some time alone together so I can concentrate on you instead.'

Helen actually felt herself blushing. He made her feel so young, almost like a schoolgirl again. 'I don't think you'll find me very interesting,' she said shyly.

'You shouldn't belittle yourself.'

They were driving through the suburbs, heading west. Ahead of them, the mountains were softened by a slight haze. 'Where are we going?'

'I don't care. A drive, a walk by the river, coffee. It's up to you.'

'I'll settle for a walk by the river,' she said happily.

He was still having trouble finding a suitable gallery. In fact, he told her that it was becoming rather sticky. 'You see, the best places are either booked up for months, or charging an arm and a leg in percentages.' But even though they were running out of options, he promised he would keep trying.

Helen was disappointed to hear this. 'Are you saying that we might have to forget the idea?'

'No, it hasn't come to that yet,' he replied. 'But I wouldn't want you to build your hopes too high. But . . . I feel terrible, promising everything and coming up with nothing.'

Helen told him not to worry about it. She had only

142

agreed to allow her paintings to be shown mainly to please her family. And, anyway, there was more to life than exhibitions.

But Douglas's pessimism was short-lived. The next day, he telephoned to say that he had found a place and wanted Helen to come and look at it. Helen was thrilled to hear it. It looked as if she would have her exhibition after all.

The gallery was small and chic. Helen was quite impressed by it. Yes, she thought, her pictures would hang very nicely on its walls.

'What happens now?'

'Now I organise the programmes and publicity.'

'But . . .'

'No, no, we can't talk about money,' he said, anticipating her protest. 'You're to leave all that to me.'

'Please, Douglas.'

'As a favour.' He smiled at her warmly. He had such an engaging smile. 'Please, Helen. I really want to do this for you.'

She didn't argue with him any further about it. All the same, her mind wasn't totally at ease.

But if he had gone to so much trouble to arrange the exhibition, then why should he have cancelled it so abruptly? It was mystifying. She had called the gallery and spoken to the woman who owned it, and whom she had met when she first visited it with Douglas. She had wanted to check the number of pictures that would be required. The woman sounded ill-at-ease. She had been friendly enough when Helen had met her. 'I'm sorry, but I don't understand,' she said. 'Your Mister Blake came in at lunch time to cancel the exhibition. I thought you knew.'

Helen hadn't known. There had been not a hint, not a whisper. She had thought everything was going along swimmingly—or at least so Douglas had kept assuring her. She was sure there had to be a perfectly reasonable explanation.

There was, he told her when she finally got through to him. He would have told her, he said, but he wanted to wait until he had found another place. He said that some difficulty had arisen with one of the partners—not the woman she had met that day and spoken to on the telephone, but the other partner, who hadn't really taken to Helen's work when he had shown it to her, which was a pity and totally misjudged—but it was his experience that unless everyone involved in running an art gallery was one hundred per cent committed to what they were displaying, then that considerably lessened the chances of the exhibition being a success. It sounded plausible enough to Helen.

'And the expense,' Douglas went on. 'You know how expensive framing is—and then there's the rental, publicity, catalogues . . . It's not a risk to be taken lightly. And I'm not just talking about money,' he went on when Helen said she was aware of that. 'One's first exhibition is extremely important. I mean, a first failure can be especially damaging, not to mention demoralising.'

Helen said she could see what he meant. 'Please understand that this is just a minor setback,' Douglas said earnestly. 'Once we've got the chemistry right, then it's all systems go.'

Helen could see his point. She told him so. She knew without doubt that he had her best interests at heart. She trusted him completely. 'I do appreciate all the thought and care you've taken in all this,' she told him when he came to visit her the next day. 'But you've made me realise that I've been approaching the whole idea of this exhibition quite unrealistically.' She had thought and thought about it during the night. 'It was quite a silly fantasy.' She held up a forestalling hand when he seemed about to protest. 'No, please, hear me out. But from what you've been telling me, once you've reached the exhibiting stage it all becomes a question of

144

money. And ego. And that's not the reason I paint, Douglas,' she said seriously. 'I paint purely for relaxation and personal pleasure.'

'Yes, but your work deserves a wider public,' Douglas said.

'But I don't deserve an ulcer. Nor do you. No, Douglas, we don't need this exhibition in order stay good friends.' She looked at him tenderly. More than anything else she wished they could remain good friends. 'Do we?'

Douglas took her hand and held it. 'Of course not.'

Helen was happy; that was just what she had wanted to hear. The fact that she wouldn't be staging an exhibition after all came as rather a relief.

It was shortly after that that Douglas suggested they take another trip into the country. He had an ulterior motive, he said; he wanted Helen's opinion on a cottage he was thinking of purchasing. He showed her the cottage. It stood on a hill above a river. It was surrounded by trees. There was an orchard behind it. Helen thought it was charming, but of course it would need to have some work done to it. 'My wife used to do all that sort of thing,' Douglas said ruefully as they walked back to the car. 'I'm hopeless at it.'

They had tramped through the small rooms of the cottage. The fireplace, in particular, was a renovator's dream, Helen had thought. 'I'll help you. If you do decide to buy it.'

Douglas beamed at her. 'That certainly puts a more favourable light on the proposition.'

There was a small guest house down by the river's edge. Douglas suggested they stop there for lunch. 'I'm glad we decided to do this today,' he said.

Helen was breathing deeply of the crisp country air. She could smell roses. 'I just wish it could go on forever. Out in the fresh air, away from the housework.'

Douglas was holding her hand. 'It *can* go on forever.'

145

Helen wasn't sure what he meant. 'What I mean is, it doesn't have to stop today. We could make a full weekend of it. Spend the night at the guest house.'

Helen looked at him doubtfully. 'I hope that's not really what it sounds like.'

Douglas shrugged. 'I suppose it depends on how you take it.'

It was too soon. 'Douglas,' she said earnestly, 'I'm sure you already know that you mean a great deal to me. But . . . you see . . . I'm not ready for anything more than the friendship we already have.'

'I know.' Douglas opened the car door for her. They faced each other across it. 'I understand completely. I had no ulterior motive, I can assure you. I did mean separate rooms.'

Of course he did. Douglas Blake was a thorough gentleman. Helen should have known all along that he had nothing else in mind than just that.

Slowly, inevitably, she was falling in love with him. He was so attentive, so thoughtful. Helen missed him when he wasn't there. She worried about him. He was in her thoughts all the time. 'When Bill died,' she said softly, 'I thought that was that. I didn't dream that I could ever find another person who could be so important to me.'

'I'm glad you did,' he said with a gentle squeeze of her hand.

They spent the weekend in the country and had a picnic lunch on the way back. By then, Helen was absolutely sure of her own mind.

'How was the weekend?' Jim Robinson asked her when she returned.

'Wonderful.' How clear everything had been—how simple and uncomplicated. Devonshire tea and long walks together. And talks—my, how they had talked. 'How was everything here?'

'Like clockwork. No problem at all.'

Helen was pleased to hear it. If the family could look after themselves . . . 'That's good,' she said with a nervous laugh. 'Because I mightn't be here for much longer.'

The smile faded from Jim's face. She knew he—the family—would be upset, but that couldn't be helped. She had her own life to lead. With Douglas. All the same, she did feel a little guilty about it.

Establishing a joint bank account seemed to her to be the most natural thing for them to do. They had talked of marriage, of a future that would see them inseparably bound together. And as a prelude to that future, they had both set their hearts on buying that cottage they had looked at in the country that day.

Douglas was handling everything. Within weeks, having settled on a date for the wedding—and being so sure of everything in her own mind, Helen didn't think they were acting too hastily—he turned up at the house with a huge bunch of flowers and the news that he had arranged everything at the Registry Office. A simple wedding was what they had decided upon, and a simple wedding was what they were getting. He also had some more exciting news. 'We'll be moving into our new home just as soon as you've chosen the furniture,' he announced gleefully.

Helen stared at him in dawning surprise and joy. 'You've bought a place?'

'I've made an offer.'

'Are you sure I'd like it?' She was really teasing him; she was certain that she would like any place that was chosen by him.

'I think you will,' he said. 'Remember that cottage in the country?'

That delightful cottage in the country, on a hill above the river. Of course she remembered it.

'It's yours.'

'Oh . . . Douglas . . .' She threw her arms around

him. She had never felt so happy in her life before.

But it seemed that the dream cottage was to remain just that. When Douglas came to the house, looking drawn and anxious and told her that he had some bad news, Helen knew it had to do with the cottage. Douglas was feeling so miserable because this was the second time he had let her down. Jim Robinson was also there; he and his partner had been working on some plans for a new engineering project when Douglas arrived.

'I never thought for a moment that I'd have any trouble selling my place in time,' Douglas said unhappily. He made a small, rueful gesture. 'But there it is. Somebody comes along with a cash offer and we're sunk.'

Helen was bitterly disappointed. She had set her heart on that little place by the river. 'But can they do this? It seems so unfair.'

'It's quite legal, I'm afraid,' Jim offered. He frowned at Douglas. 'But what about bridging finance? You could use your own house as collateral.'

'No, I can't.' Douglas sadly shook his head. 'I put in an application a couple of days ago, but they knocked me back.' He smiled thinly. 'At my age, I'm not a good risk.'

'That's nonsense,' Helen snorted.

Douglas regarded her sadly. 'But you had your heart set on it . . .'

All the plans they had made, all the things they felt they could do to make that cottage a real home for them. 'I still have you,' Helen said tenderly.

'Yes, it *is* a blow,' Jim observed quietly. 'And you only needed the money for a couple of weeks, didn't you?'

'Until I sell my place,' Douglas replied. 'Yes, that's right.'

Jim was looking very thoughtful. The following

evening, he had some news for her. 'That cottage of yours. You and Douglas can go ahead now. I happen to have found a spare fifty-eight grand.'

Helen didn't believe him. She thought he was joking—and in rather poor taste at that. 'Very funny, Jim,' she said sourly.

'Not funny,' he said. 'It happens to be true.'

But it *couldn't* . . . Helen stared at him incredulously. 'Where did it come from?'

'Secret Swiss bank account.'

'No. Seriously.' She was losing patience. Honestly, he could be like a kid sometimes with his silly clowning. 'What have you been up to? Have you mortgaged the house.' She shook her head. 'If you have, I can't let you do it.'

'It's nothing like that.' He was being perfectly serious now. He had just come home from the office. Helen had been fixing dinner—and there wouldn't be many more dinners she would be fixing for this family of hers on a regular basis. 'It's a regular loan from the company. Ross Warner is quite happy with the collateral. And, anyway, the money is just sitting there, doing nothing.'

She knew the money had been earmarked for their new project. 'I can't accept it, Jim,' she said flatly.

'Why not?' Jim looked pained. 'Ross is quite happy for you and Douglas to have it. And it's only for a couple of weeks. You pay the money back, and we're still in the black. So . . .' he spread his hands in a gesture of appeal . . . 'what's wrong with that?'

He was only trying to help, and Helen felt bad about having to disappoint him. 'Never borrow from family or friends.' She realised she was sounding a little prim as she said it. 'It's a sure way to lose them.'

'Oh, come *on*, Helen.' There was an aggrieved edge to Jim's voice. 'You want the cottage, and now you can have it. What's wrong with that? And I want to help.'

Helen knew he did. 'I'm grateful, Jim, believe me. But I just can't accept it. I'm sure Douglas would agree with me.'

But Douglas didn't agree with her, she learned when she discovered him and Jim having an earnest conversation in the living room later that evening. She had heard the doorbell, and had thought it was someone for Jim or for one of the kids. Then she had heard Douglas's voice. She was angry with Jim, who had obviously been in touch with Douglas behind her back.

'He's right, you know,' Douglas said. 'We should at least talk it over.'

She gave him a withering look. Jim made some excuse to leave them alone. 'Let me know when you've reached a decision,' he said.

They were both ganging up on her, Helen thought resentfully. It wasn't fair. 'So what's wrong with Jim's offer?' Douglas was sitting beside her on the couch, holding her hand. 'It seems very generous to me.'

'It just wouldn't be right,' Helen said. 'That money's vital to the company. What would happen if we couldn't pay it back?' She had to think of the worst.

But Douglas had an answer for that as well. 'We could fix it up legally. My solicitor can draw up the papers, we set a fair rate of interest, use my place as collateral—and then there's the cottage, too, as added security. What can go wrong?'

Helen wasn't sure. She knew very little about this sort of thing. 'It just doesn't *feel* right. It's too close, too personal.'

Douglas was watching her eagerly. 'But if I put it all in *my* name? If *I* take the loan? Would *that* make you feel any better? Or don't you trust me to handle our affairs?'

Perhaps it *would* make her feel better. She laughed and laid her head on the comfortable pad of his shoulder. Bending his head over her, he kissed her— and that *did* make her feel better.

So the loan was arranged. Helen could go ahead with her plans for the cottage. There would be masses of roses in the garden. It was just too good to be true.

The contracts were signed. The terms were quite simple. Douglas had to pay the money to the real estate agent, while Jim and his partner had the cottage as collateral for the loan. They celebrated in French champagne Jim had bought especially for the occasion.

On the day he told her the purchase of the cottage was to be finalised, Helen accompanied Douglas to the bank. By the time the bank cheque to cover the purchase had been made out to Douglas's solicitor, there was only fourteen dollars left in their joint bank account. 'What happens now?' Helen asked him.

'I have to sign a few papers, hand the cheque over to Royston—and the house is ours.' He grinned at her in delight.

Helen smiled happily back at him. She had quite forgotten how exciting it was to buy a new house.

They stood outside the bank. Helen was on her way to an appointment with her hairdresser. Douglas kissed her and turned away. Fondly, Helen watched him until he had turned the corner. All they needed to do now was to be married in a simple ceremony at the Registry Office. It still seemed so unreal, a fairytale . . .

When Jim came home that evening, she was trying on the dress she had bought for the wedding—dark green and simple, but how young and fresh it made her look. 'What do you think of it?' Helen greeted him in the hall. 'My wedding dress.' Then, noticing his expression, her smile faded. He was looking very upset about something.

'I'm sorry, Helen,' he said gravely. 'But there's not going to be a wedding.'

Another of his jokes? No. He was much too serious to be joking. Helen stared at him uncomprehendingly. 'What . . . what do you mean? No wedding?' Something had happened. 'What was it? Douglas? Has there been an accident.'

'I think you should sit down, Helen.'

She shook her head. 'Tell me what's happened.' No wedding? It was unbelievable. Everything had been arranged, the date had been fixed, and Helen had bought a new dress.

'Helen . . . look . . .' He raised his hand then let it drop to his side again. He looked totally defeated. 'Douglas conned all of us.'

'*What?*'

'It's true, Helen. The company's solicitor rang me this morning. He had tried to contact Douglas's solicitor, this man Royston he told us about . . . but he doesn't exist.'

There had to be a simple explanation. 'He probably made a mistake about the name, or the address,' Helen said quickly. 'A lapse of memory. Surely there's nothing criminal about that.'

'He's gone, Helen. He's cleared out. I went around to his place, but there's no one there.'

No . . . It was cruel. The things Douglas had told her, the plans they had made . . . She knew suddenly that Jim was telling her the truth, that there was no mistake, a simple memory lapse. Douglas had gone— and he had taken all that money with him. 'Oh my God,' she moaned, turning away in the simple green dress she had bought for her wedding.

Eleven

This was the woman who had walked the Hindu Kush, ridden a camel across the Empty Quarter and told Mussolini to his face that he was behaving like a petulant schoolboy; who had lived with Dyak tribesmen in the jungles of Borneo and gone to the races with the Aga Khan, had sweltered in the Amazon, had been shipwrecked, and taken an active part in a number of different wars. The inveterate traveller who had interviewed statesmen, crooked financiers and military dictators. A woman of the world, an adventuress who treated danger with her usual disdain. Jim Robinson had mixed feelings about having his mother stay with them. She was so much larger than life, quite overpowering.

Where did she say she had just come from ? Mongolia? Tibet? Now, with all her cameras and recorders, notebooks and other paraphernalia, she had just arrived in Ramsay Street. Of course the kids were thrilled to have her there. It was almost five years since they had last seen her.

Young Scott was particularly pleased; he had already decided to write a profile of his grandmother for his English Expression class. She would be an ideal subject, he thought. 'I'd like to do a proper interview,' he told her at the dinner table that night. 'With photographs.'

'I don't think Nan came all this way to be interviewed by you, Julie told him rather huffily. 'Besides, at her age, she wants to take it easy.'

'Nonsense, girl.' Despite her grey hair and lined face, Bess Robinson had the carriage and vigour of a woman many years her junior. 'I'd be delighted.'

Scott looked pleased. 'I've been keeping a scrapbook. Articles and interviews. Would you like to see it?'

'Of course I would.'

Jim looked at his mother, who looked as if she had just walked all the way from Borneo, or Tibet—or perhaps it was somewhere in Africa; the woman just never kept still. 'Why don't you relax, Mum? Put your feet up.'

Bess smiled fondly at her son. 'My darling boy,' she said in that deep brisk voice of hers. 'When have you known me to do that?'

Never. But then he hardly knew *her*, what with all the gadding about across the earth's surface, dodging bullets and catching marlin off the Florida coast.

'I just hope Scott doesn't wear her out,' Julie remarked after Scott had borne his mother off to his room.

'I doubt it,' Jim said with a grim smile.

Julie was working on some tapestry. She looked sharply up at her father. 'You don't seem very pleased to have her here.'

'It's just that she makes me nervous,' Jim said after a moment's reflection. 'She's lived such an exciting life. She's one of a kind.' He wasn't quite sure if the world shouldn't be grateful for that.

'All the same,' Julie mused. 'It must have been an interesting childhood for you.'

Bess knew more about Tuareg tribesmen than her own son. 'She was hardly ever there more than a few weeks at a time. Aunt Daisy more or less brought me up.' His mother's brief appearances were more like whirlwinds that were just as suddenly gone again, leaving a trail of havoc behind. 'Oh, I was well cared for,' he said. 'I had more doting aunts than you could poke a stick at.'

'Then you must have resented her for not being there,' Julie observed shrewdly.

Jim thought about that. 'Perhaps I did. Perhaps that's why I've always been so determined to make sure my own kids had a stable upbringing.'

Just before she turned in for the night, his mother found Jim in the living room where he was watching television. 'You haven't asked me how long I intend staying,' she said.

'I didn't think it was necessary. You know you're welcome to stay as long as you like.'

'I don't believe you.' She laughed. 'But I'll be out of your hair in a day or two. I didn't come to town just to see *you*, you know.'

Of course not, Jim thought grimly; she never had. 'Silly of me to presume you had,' he said.

'Why must you always take me so seriously?'

Who *was* this woman who had flown planes and drunk Hemingway under the table in Madrid? His mother, whom he hardly knew. 'Perhaps I don't have a sense of humour.' Pushing himself up out of his chair, he moved into the kitchen where he filled the electric jug and switched it on.

'You've done a very good job with that younger son of yours,' she said, following him into the kitchen.

'Scott?' Jim nodded. He thought so, too. 'Yes, you two seem to hit it off very nicely.'

'I'd like to take him out tomorrow. There's a film showing at the Museum which would be very useful to him in his English Expression project.'

'It's a school day tomorrow,' he reminded her.

Obviously, she and Scott had already discussed this. 'I know, but a great strapping lad like that can miss one game of football. And he has free study in the morning.'

'He needs all the study he can get.'

'He can make up the time. He said he could.'

She was being persuasive. She was working on him.

155

'Please don't do this to me, Mum,' he groaned.

'Come on, Jim, be reasonable,' said this woman in probably the same tone she had told Mussolini not to *sulk*. 'That lad has paid me an enormous compliment, and I would like to do something for him in return.'

He could never resist her, and disliked himself because of it. The water was boiling. He switched off the jug. 'Who am I to argue with your . . . logic?' he queried with a resigned shrug of his shoulders.

When Scott was awarded top marks for the essay he had written on his grandmother, and with Bess sharing his excitement, Jim felt strangely excluded. More so when, with Bess's encouragement, the boy decided he wanted to write a book about his famous grandmother who had once exchanged jokes with President Roosevelt. 'It would be a best seller,' she suggested happily and without a trace of modesty. Curious, Jim began to read the essay which Scott had left on the table beside his chair.

'Bess Robinson has managed to carve out a career for herself in a profession mainly dominated by men, despite the handicap of having a small child . . .' That was as far as he got. He didn't like the way Scott was seeing him as some sort of encumbrance to a free-ranging soul, which was something he certainly hadn't been. Bess just would not allow any encumbrances. He tossed the essay back onto the table.

'What did you think of my essay?' Scott asked him at breakfast the following morning.

'I'm sorry.' Jim was feeling a little guilty. 'I haven't had a chance to read it yet.'

'That's okay,' Scott said coolly. 'It only took me two weeks to write it.'

Jim was stung by the sarcasm. 'I just couldn't get to it last night.'

'Sure, Dad,' Jim knew his son was disappointed. 'Some other time then.'

'What do you mean, you didn't have a chance to read it?' Helen Daniels challenged him after Scott had set off for school. Bess hadn't yet come down for breakfast. Lucy had also been packed off to school, and Paul was on a flight to Singapore or somewhere.

'You've read it, Helen.' Jim glowered up at his mother-in-law from the breakfast table. 'How would you like to be described as a handicap to your mother's career?'

Helen looked at him in astonishment. 'You must be joking.'

Jim tried to remember the opening lines of Scott's essay. 'How does it go? Yes. "In a world dominated by men . . ." I was one of the men involved.'

'You were only a child.'

'Exactly.'

'Scott didn't mean to hurt your feelings,' Helen said. 'I'm sure he's not even aware of what they are.'

The memories were not altogether pleasant. 'I was brought up by a bunch of feminists who also weren't aware of my feelings,' he said resentfully. 'All that mattered was my mother's career.' What was it she had actually said to Kemal Ataturk? Something that was always being quoted. 'To hell with how I felt about not having a mother.'

'She did the best for you, Jim,' Helen said quietly.

'Maybe she did.' But how much was best? A philosophical question. Jim was still remembering. 'Instead of bedtime stories, all I had were those that had my mother's byline. Narrow escapes from pygmies with poisoned darts, an on-the-spot report from an earthquake-devastated town.' He sighed. 'Everybody told me how lucky I was to have such a brave and famous mother. Not that it was much use to me.'

Helen was watching him with an expression of concern. 'Is that why you married Anne?'

Anne . . . She shouldn't have died. She had been

much too young to die. And there was his mother, dicing with death every step every step of the long and perilous way. It was an irony. 'I married Anne because I loved her,' he said tightly. 'All she was interested in was having a family and staying at home to bring them up. Is there anything wrong with that?'

'No, of course not. But not all women have the same outlook.'

'Fine, fine.' Jim gestured impatiently. 'It was just hard on me, not having a father—and newsprint for a mother.'

'Does that mean you're ashamed of her?' Helen asked.

'Of course I'm not ashamed of her,' Jim said forcefully. 'It's just that I don't know who she is.' A fugitive from the pygmies, the bane of Mussolini.

'Then read Scott's essay,' Helen suggested.

'All right,' he said grudgingly. 'I will.'

Helen made more tea while he read the essay. He had to admit it was very good. It was very informative. His mother in the front line, ducking the bullets, trudging bravely over Macedonian mountain tops. But it didn't mean that his feelings towards her had changed.

That day he bought his son a typewriter. He thought the boy needed all the encouragement he could get. Scott was overjoyed. Now, he said, he could begin to work on his grandmother's biography in earnest.

Bess had plenty to do now she was back in town. She was spending most of her days away from the house. In the meantime, Scott was getting himself organised for the task in hand. Bess had given him a mass of material which needed to be sorted.

After some days, it became increasingly clear to Jim that there was something worrying Scott. Bess had already announced that as her business had almost been completed, she would be moving on within the next few days. She had said something about the Solomon Islands. Helen arranged to cook a special farewell dinner for her on her last night. It so happened that at the same time, Jim had arranged to be out of town on a business trip. He didn't think it mattered if he wasn't there for this farewell dinner. Scott was horrified. 'But you *can't* go,' he protested. 'You'll have to put it off.'

'I can't put it off,' Jim told him. 'Anyway, why is it so important? She'll be back again.' From the Solomon Islands, from the Yukon and Yucatan.

'But you've *got* to be here,' Scott cried.

Jim couldn't understand why his son was being so insistent. 'I'm sure you can cope very nicely without me,' he said emphatically. 'I'm sorry, but I won't be there.'

'You don't understand.' The boy seemed genuinely distressed. Jim was puzzled. 'This is really serious.'

Was there something going on that Jim didn't know about? 'What do you mean—really serious?'

Scott became hesitant. 'It's just that I don't think you should be going when Nanna's about to leave, that's all. Can't you at least wait until she's gone?'

Jim couldn't. He was becoming impatient. 'This is business.'

'You don't care about her, do you?' Scott accused him.

'Of course I care about her,' Jim replied tersely. 'She's my mother.' He looked closely at his son. 'Is there something you haven't told me?'

'No.' It seemed to Jim that Scott was suddenly evasive. There was something definitely worrying him. 'I just think we should have a farewell dinner for Nan, that's all.'

'And I'm saying I can't be there.' His mother was irrepressible; she would be back. She had always had her own way. 'She has never changed her plans to suit my needs,' he said with some bitterness, 'and I'm not about to change mine to suit hers. She wouldn't expect it of me. Besides . . .' he gave a short, dry laugh . . .' she won't even notice that I'm not there.'

'Please, Dad . . .'

There was no use arguing any more. Enough had been said. Bess would be happy among the natives of the Solomon Islands. 'No, Scott,' he said with grim finality. 'No way. I won't be here—and that's it.'

He did find out what was wrong—and it was almost too late. His mother was a dying woman. Scott knew—but it wasn't Scott who told him. It was Bess's last day in town. Jim had left for the office early because there were a few things that needed to be attended to there before he caught the afternoon plane. He had planned to come home first and pack a few things for his trip, but when Helen told him that Bess would be out that afternoon, he had called her from the office to wish her all the best. It was a rather short and stilted conversation, and Jim felt somewhat guilty that he should be relieved when it was over. But he knew he would see her again. She would bounce back full of life from the Solomon Islands.

And now he knew she wouldn't. He had just finished packing his bag and was about to leave the house when there was a knock at the front door. He opened it to see a grey-haired man in a dark suit standing on the doorstep.

'Oh, I was wondering if I could see Bess Robinson.'

'She's not here at the moment.'

'Then you must be Jim Robinson.'

'That's right.' Jim was a little puzzled as to who this stranger might be. A professional man of some sort, he guessed. A doctor? He was carrying a briefcase.

'My name's Edward Wigram,' the man said, holding out his hand. 'I'm your mother's solicitor. She may have mentioned me . . .'

She hadn't. Jim shook hands with his mother's solicitor. 'I'm sorry . . .'

'No, probably not.' Wigram smiled. 'You don't see a great deal of each other, do you? I mean, Bess and her ceaseless travels . . . there wouldn't be the opportunity.' His smile was quite warm and friendly. Jim was curious as to why his mother's solicitor should suddenly turn up on the doorstep without any warning. 'Your mother and I are also very good friends. I've known her for more years than either of us would care to remember.'

Jim opened the door wider and stepped to one side. 'Please, come in.'

The solicitor nodded his thanks and moved into the hallway. Closing the door behind him, Jim ushered him into the living room. 'How can I help you?'

Resting his briefcase on the table, Wigram opened it. 'I've got some papers here for Bess to sign.' He extracted the papers from the briefcase, quite a sheaf of them, then looked gravely at Jim. 'They totally slipped my mind yesterday when I saw her. It was the . . . shock, I think.'

The shock? Jim had no idea what the man was talking about. 'If you'd like to leave them. She'll be back this evening.'

'They *are* rather confidential . . .'

'I can make sure she gets them,' Jim said. 'I won't be here myself, but I can leave a note. It's no problem,' he added as he noted Wigram's worried frown.

'If you're sure . . .' Wigram still seemed reluctant. 'In normal circumstances I wouldn't have called personally. But I was hoping to see her again, you see.' He seemed curiously uncertain about something. 'Just once more. I'm going to miss her,' he said with a sigh.

'Yes, we all will,' Jim said.

Wigram nodded solemnly. 'It must be a terrible shock to the family.' Jim looked at him. It had never been a shock before; Bess just came and went. 'I believe your son is taking the news very hard.'

Well, Scott was fond of his grandmother, naturally. 'Yeah . . . well, like I said, we'll all miss her.'

Wigram was shaking his head in wonderment. 'I still can't come to terms with it,' he said sadly. 'All that life and energy . . . just disappearing.' Disappearing into mountain ranges and tents that were made of yak hair. Out there on the great silk road to China. 'I thought she would live forever.'

Jim just didn't understand what this was all about. 'I'm sorry?'

'Her illness.' Wigram regarded him quizzically. 'Surely she told you about it?' Jim felt suddenly numb. Oh no . . . no Bess. Wigram was full of apologies. 'She didn't . . . oh dear, I'm sorry. I naturally assumed . . . when she said her grandson knew . . . he had found a letter among her papers, apparently . . . from her doctor.' He was genuinely distressed. He fidgeted with the clasp of his briefcase. 'I hope I haven't broken any confidences.'

That was the way it would have happened, Jim thought unhappily after Wigram had gone. She would have sworn Scott to secrecy after he had discovered her secret which had been inadvertently left among all those papers she had passed over to him. That would have been just like Bess—and that was why Scott had been so upset that his father wouldn't be there for the farewell dinner. Farewell . . . The word had taken on a new and tragic meaning. Farewell. A life so rich and full—and now, to come to an end. Farewell indeed.

His bag was packed. His plane would leave in just over an hour. He came to a decision. The plane would have to go without him. His bag would have to be unpacked. He would see his mother one last time before she embarked on the greatest adventure of all. He crossed to the telephone.

Twelve

It was the beef Max was having with Danny's French teacher that brought it all to a head. If he hadn't decided to help Danny with his French essay then Danny wouldn't have heard the conversation behind the potted palms which was to shatter the conception he had of himself and bring him a great deal of unhappiness.

The thing was, Max spoke French rather well. He had picked it up here and there, but mainly from Maria's father, Danny's maternal grandfather, whose European background had brought him into contact with a number of languages. 'I'll give you a hand,' he offered.

Danny had been struggling with his French essay. He welcomed the help because French was something . . . well, it was all Greek to him. Sitting himself at the table, Max drew up a pad and pen. 'Now what will I write about?' He considered the blank page in front of him. 'I know. Plumbing. I've got that right down to my fingertips. Interesting, too.'

Danny looked at him askance. 'Plumbing?' he groaned. 'You'll give me away.'

'Well, what then?'

'Girls. Or rock music.'

'Don't be silly.' Max picked up the pen. 'I want to get top marks, don't I? I'll think of something suitable.'

'I trust you, Dad,' Danny said.

'I know,' Max said again, beginning to write. '*Ma Vacance*.'

But Max's vacation—the beach, seagulls, and Danny had had to stop him rapturising over the bar of the seaside pub where, in fact, he had spent most of his time—didn't draw the expected response from Miss Drew, the French teacher. 'Come on, tell me,' Max demanded impatiently when Danny brought the result home. It was a moment Danny had been dreading; his father had to be top in everything, even in French—and this was something he had proved not to be.

'Fifteen.'

'Ah.' Max grinned broadly and clapped his hands together. 'Fifteen, eh? Out of twenty. That's pretty good.'

Pretty bad, actually. 'Out of a hundred,' Danny said glumly, and waited for the explosion.

'What do you mean?' Max glared at him belligerently. 'Out of a hundred?'

'It means you failed.' Danny wished there was some other way he could have broken the news—preferably with him not being there to face his father's outrage.

Max's face was twisted in a fearsome scowl. '*What?*'

'You did better than I would have,' Danny hastily tried to reassure him.

'But Max wasn't reassured. A mortal blow had been struck. 'No one fails me and gets away with it,' he bellowed like a wounded bull. 'I'm going to write that teacher of yours a letter. She'll rue the day.'

He wrote the letter, and in the morning instructed Danny to hand it to his teacher. His teacher also wrote a letter and instructed Danny to hand it to his father. Max's face turned a shade of crimson as he read it. It wasn't the written apology he had expected. 'This is *obscene*,' he yelled. 'She's called me "*un grenouille gros*".'

'What does that mean?'

'A fat frog. And she had twigged that it was me who wrote the letter—not you.'

Danny wasn't surprised. 'That figures.'

'That's as may be,' Max said indignantly. 'But she can't say that sort of thing to a parent.'

'It depends on what you put in *your* letter,' Danny pointed out to him.

'A few home truths, that's all,' Max muttered savagely.

'Why don't you just forget it, Dad?' It was all very embarrassing for Danny.

'No, I won't,' Max retorted. 'I'll show the old bat. Just you wait.'

Danny wouldn't have exactly called his French teacher an old bat. Miss Drew was quite young, really.

When he heard that his father had been on the telephone to Miss Drew, Danny was dismayed. Max sounded eminently pleased with himself. He had told her a thing or two, giving him marks like that when he could speak and write French as well as any Frenchman could do. Fat frog indeed.

It threatened to be an ongoing battle. But when, a few days later, Max happened to mention, quite casually, that Miss Drew wouldn't be at school that day, and Shane had looked at him dubiously and said she was always there, rain, hail or shine, Max laughed and said, 'Not when there's free plumbing on offer. It seemed that a truce had been called.

'What have you done, Dad?' Danny asked suspiciously.

'I've just made a deal with her,' Max happily informed him. 'She re-marks my essay, and I fix the knock in her pipes. A quid pro quo—and Bob *est ton oncle.*'

He must have fixed her points. From that point on, Miss Drew seemed to be treating him with less severity. Max began to take to wearing a scarf and whistling 'Frère Jacques' or 'La Marseillaise'. He became secretive about his movements. Sometimes Danny could smell his aftershave, or the garlic on his breath when he came in the evening looking highly pleased with himself.

There was something strange about Shane Robinson's behaviour when Danny and his older brother, Shane, went down to the coffee shop for dinner that night. Max had said he was going out, was dressed up to the nines, and his aftershave was more pervasive than ever. Scott, who was working at the coffee shop, seemed to be on edge, hovering close to their table as he waited to take their order. Then Danny saw why he was behaving like that. Sitting at a table on the other side of the potted palms, was his father—and Miss Drew. Danny was curious. He stood up, and moved towards the potted palms. 'Leave them alone, Danny,' Shane warned him.

It was a warning he should have heeded. If he hadn't moved across to the potted palms to eavesdrop on his father and Miss Drew, deep in conversation, Max smelling of aftershave and Miss Drew staring intently in his eyes as she told him he shouldn't blame himself, he wouldn't have heard Max say, 'But I do. I mean, there are still things he doesn't know about. But I still can't bring myself to tell him.'

He wouldn't have heard Miss Drew—her first name was Kate—say, 'If there's one thing I know from all my years of teaching, is that there's no such thing as family secrets. The kids always know.'

Or Max deliver his bombshell. 'But Danny doesn't know. You see, I'm not his father.'

If, motivated by his curiosity, a sense of fun—of mischief even, perhaps surprising Max and Kate by springing out from behind the potted palms—he could have gone on believing what he had always believed; that despite all his setbacks, Max was his father and that his family was his real one.

The worst of it was, he realised later after the shock had worn off and was replaced by a smouldering anger, that everyone else seemed to know about. Only *he* was the one who didn't know. Shane knew. 'So you tell me,' Danny demanded after they had returned to the house in gloomy silence. 'Where is my real family?'

'We are, of course.'

'I'm not stupid,' Danny yelled at him. 'If Max isn't my father, who is?'

'I don't know.'

'Then they adopted me—is that it?'

Shane shook his head. 'You really should speak to Dad about this.'

'Why should I?' Danny was pacing up and down. He was very agitated. 'If he's not my father . . .' And that did explain a lot of things, Max's attitude towards him, all the shouting, the rejection Danny had so often felt. 'All those years he was yelling at me. Now I find out he's not even my father. And Mum . .?' She had left them. She had met another man and gone to Hong Kong. The family . . . what was left of it . . . Danny could feel the tears stinging in his eyes.

'Of course, she's your mother,' Shane said. 'And I'm your brother. Now just calm down.'

But Danny couldn't calm down. 'Is that why they split up? Over me?'

Shane nodded. 'That was when I found out. And Dad moved out of the house.' His eyes pleaded with Danny. 'I thought of telling you. Honestly. But it was all settling down, and Dad was accepting you . . . at last . . . and everything . . .'

'I *won't* accept him, Shane,' Danny cried, flinging himself out of the room. 'I *can't*. He's not . . . my father.'

He lay on his bed, in the darkness staring up at the ceiling, confused, miserable, so many things swirling around inside his head. He didn't know how long he had been lying there when the door opened. He blinked in the sudden rush of light. His father . . . no, not his father, Danny reminded himself . . . Max was standing in the doorway. 'You all right?'

167

'Does it matter?' Danny refused to look at him.

Max advanced into the room a few steps then hesitated. 'Shane told me what's bothering you . . . and I'm sorry you had to find out the way you did. I've been thinking . . . and I just want you to know . . . You're still my son. Like Shane . . . and as long as you live here, this is your home . . . and I'm your father. I know I yell at you, and we fight . . . but that's the way we are. And underneath it all, I love you, son. Please believe me, Danny. Please . . .'

Slowly, very slowly, Danny's eyes moved down from the ceiling to his father who was standing near his bed, his eyes moist, one arm outstretched in entreaty, and a hopeful smile on his lips.

STAR BOOKS BESTSELLERS

	TESSA BARCLAY	
0352315520	**Garland of War**	£1.95
0352317612	**The Wine Widow**	£2.50
0352304251	**A Sower Went Forth**	£2.25
0352308060	**The Stony Places**	£2.25
0352313331	**Harvest of Thorns**	£2.25
0352315857	**The Good Ground**	£1.95
035231687X	**Champagne Girls**	£2.95
	JOANNA BARNES	
0352316969	**Silverwood**	£3.25
	LOIS BATTLE	
035231270X	**War Brides**	£2.75*
0352316640	**Southern Women**	£2.95*

STAR Books are obtainable from many booksellers and newsagents. If you have any difficulty tick the titles you want and fill in the form below.

Name _____

Address _____

_____

Send to: Star Books Cash Sales, P.O. Box 11, Falmouth, Cornwall, TR10 9EN.

Please send a cheque or postal order to the value of the cover price plus:
UK: 55p for the first book, 22p for the second book and 14p for each additional book ordered to the maximum charge of £1.75.

BFPO and EIRE: 55p for the first book, 22p for the second book, 14p per copy for the next 7 books, thereafter 8p per book.

OVERSEAS: £1.00 for the first book and 25p per copy for each additional book.

While every effort is made to keep prices low, it is sometimes necessary to increase prices at short notice. Star Books reserve the right to show new retail prices on covers which may differ from those advertised in the text or elsewhere.

*NOT FOR SALE IN CANADA

STAR BOOKS BESTSELLERS

STAR Books are obtainable from many booksellers and newsagents. If you have any difficulty tick the titles you want and fill in the form below.

Name _____

Address _____

_____

Send to: Star Books Cash Sales, P.O. Box 11, Falmouth, Cornwall, TR10 9EN.

Please send a cheque or postal order to the value of the cover price plus: UK: 55p for the first book, 22p for the second book and 14p for each additional book ordered to the maximum charge of £1.75.

BFPO and EIRE: 55p for the first book, 22p for the second book, 14p per copy for the next 7 books, thereafter 8p per book.

OVERSEAS: £1.00 for the first book and 25p per copy for each additional book.

While every effort is made to keep prices low, it is sometimes necessary to increase prices at short notice. Star Books reserve the right to show new retail prices on covers which may differ from those advertised in the text or elsewhere.

*NOT FOR SALE IN CANADA

STAR BOOKS BESTSELLERS

FRANÇOISE SAGAN

0352314834	The Painted Lady	£2.25*
035231611X	The Still Storm	£1.95*
035231690X	The Unmade Bed	£2.25*
0352317272	Incidental Music	£2.00*
0352317914	Le Chien Couchant	£1.95*

RICHARD BEN SAPIR

0352315121	The Body	£2.50*
0352316748	Bressio	£2.50*
0352315970	Spies	£2.50*

STANLEY SHAW

0362315903	Sherlock Holmes at the 1902 Fifth Test	£1.95

IRENE SHUBIK

0352319941	The War Guest	£1.95

STAR BOOKS BESTSELLERS

STAR Books are obtainable from many booksellers and newsagents. If you have any difficulty tick the titles you want and fill in the form below.

Name _____

Address _____

_____

Send to: Star Books Cash Sales, P.O. Box 11, Falmouth, Cornwall, TR10 9EN.

Please send a cheque or postal order to the value of the cover price plus: UK: 55p for the first book, 22p for the second book and 14p for each additional book ordered to the maximum charge of £1.75.

BFPO and EIRE: 55p for the first book, 22p for the second book, 14p per copy for the next 7 books, thereafter 8p per book.

OVERSEAS: £1.00 for the first book and 25p per copy for each additional book.

While every effort is made to keep prices low, it is sometimes necessary to increase prices at short notice. Star Books reserve the right to show new retail prices on covers which may differ from those advertised in the text or elsewhere.

*NOT FOR SALE IN CANADA